ACROSS A WAR-TOSSED SEA

L. M. Elliott

DISNEY • HYPERION BOOKS
NEW YORK

 For information address Disney • Hyperion Books, 125 West End Avenue, New York, New York 10023.

Printed in the United States of America
First Edition
1 3 5 7 9 10 8 6 4 2

G475-5664-5-14015

Originally broadcast on CBS World News on December 3, 1943
over the CBS Radio Network.

Library of Congress Cataloging-in-Publication Data
Elliott, Laura, 1957–
Across a war-tossed sea/L.M. Elliott.—First edition.
pages cm
Summary: "Two British brothers adjust to life in Virginia after escaping the Blitz during World War II"—Provided by publisher.
ISBN 978-1-4231-5755-7 (hardback)
1. World War, 1939–1945—Evacuation of civilians—Great Britain—Juvenile fiction. [1. World War, 1939–1945—Evacuation of civilians—Fiction. 2. World War, 1939–1945—United States—Fiction. 3. Brothers—Fiction. 4. British—United States—Fiction. 5. Richmond (Va.)—History—20th century—Fiction.] I. Title.
PZ7.E453Ac 2014
[Fic]—dc23 2013035303

Reinforced binding

Visit www.DisneyBooks.com

THIS LABEL APPLIES TO TEXT STOCK

For Peter and Megan,
my beacons in the voyage

Chapter One

Labor Day, 1943, just east of Richmond, Virginia

"Call the watch! Lower a lifeboat! The waves will swallow them up soon!" Wesley Bishop shouted. "Hurry!"

"Wes, are you daft?" Charles shook his younger brother's arm to quiet him. "Stop blithering!"

Charles Bishop sat back on his heels and scanned Wesley's face, trying to gauge if he was awake. Wesley's blue eyes were wide open, but clearly he was imagining a very different place from the shady pond where he and Charles were celebrating Labor Day with their American host family.

"We've got to do something!" Wesley shouted again. He pointed at the Ratcliff boys shoving sheets of water at each other amid good-natured teasing. "They'll drown if we don't! Don't you see them?"

Charles recognized Wesley's sleep-talking daze all too well.

Nightmares had hounded him ever since he and Charles had sailed the Atlantic Ocean to escape Hitler's nightly bombing of England—horrendous dreams about exploding firebombs hitting their London borough, about Nazi submarines torpedoing their ship convoy, about drowning in the war-tossed sea. Usually Charles could silence the ten-year-old before he woke up the Ratcliffs with his nighttime outbursts. But here they were at the swimming hole with all five Ratcliff siblings and in broad daylight!

"Wes," Charles said, taking him by the shoulders. "Wake up. Look at me!"

Wesley quieted.

Awkwardly, Charles patted his arm. "There, you see, Wes, nothing but a bad dream."

He always felt so at sea himself when Wesley had these nightmares. Since crossing three thousand miles of ocean and settling in on the Ratcliff farm, Charles had had to play dad, mum, and big brother all to Wesley. Truth be known, Charles was rather homesick himself. No one comforted him when he was racked with similar nightmares!

Besides, hadn't the British officials who'd herded them and dozens of other child evacuees onto the ocean liner instructed them to "never show they were downhearted," so they'd be good "little ambassadors" for England? Blubbering certainly wasn't the way to do that. And it certainly wasn't the way to impress hardy American farm boys like the Ratcliffs.

Charles squared his shoulders. Mimicking the stiff-upper-lip adults he'd grown up listening to in England, the fourteen-year-old adopted a tone of voice designed to prompt agreement: "All righty, then, Wes?"

Wesley nodded.

Relieved, Charles flopped down onto the bank's velvety moss to watch the Ratcliffs swim in the deep pond that fed Four Mile Creek before it emptied into the James River. The pond was an oasis of coolness and playtime, an escape from their daily chores, and the family's favorite place on earth. The siblings hurried there whenever possible. Even on that sizzling afternoon, the Ratcliff boys had raced each other across frying-pan-hot fields, whooping and hollering, to see who'd reach the pond first, the corn popping with panicked grasshoppers jumping out of their way. There'd been no proper rain in Virginia for forty-one days straight, and all the farmers' corn had shriveled to brown stalks. The air was so hot it almost felt too thick to breathe.

Despite that, Charles had kept apace with the American-rowdy clan, as usual. But Wesley had walked behind with the Ratcliffs' older sister, Patsy, who lugged a basket crammed with sandwiches and bottles of Royal Crown Cola. As soon as they reached the dark-green gloom of the woods, Wesley had lain down and fallen asleep, worn out by the heat. Charles had plunged into the pond with the Ratcliff boys, scrambling out only at the sound of Wesley's first whimper.

Now Charles decided to stay by Wesley on the sidelines of the fun. He laughed as the youngest Ratcliffs—the seven-year-old twins, Johnny and Jamie—dunked each other. Their roughhousing reminded him of his and Wesley's corgi puppies back home. "Very like Hamlet and Horatio, eh, Wes?" Charles elbowed his little brother, trying to pull him into conversation, away from his bad memories.

That was a mistake.

Something about the boys' happy thrashing set Wesley off again. "There! Another hit! Another ship's going down!" Wesley cried out, gesturing wildly at the twins, then at the older boys, Bobby and Ron. "Throw them life preservers! Quick, oh quick!"

With this outburst, Charles knew the exact origin of Wesley's hallucination. He was reliving the night Nazi submarines, called U-boats, torpedoed nine ships in their convoy. The explosions had hurled hundreds of souls into the angry, freezing Atlantic.

"Blimey, Wes," Charles hissed. "Put a sock in it!" At this point, Charles was desperate to quiet him before the others heard.

But it was too late. Patsy was already climbing off the tree swing where she'd been reading and writing in a big notebook. She hurried toward them, her heart-shaped face awash with concern.

"Wesley, honey, what's the matter?"

At the sound of Patsy's soft Tidewater drawl, Wesley shuddered. He blinked. His eyes cleared. He looked at Patsy, then at Charles, then back to Patsy. "Sorry," he mumbled. "I'm terribly sorry." He rubbed away a tear.

"What were you dreaming about, sugar?" Patsy took Wesley's hand and brushed his blond curls back from his forehead.

Worrying how Wesley might answer, Charles jumped in:

"Oh, it was nothing much. Just some rubbish about our trip over." He cued his brother with a little nod to get him to follow his lead.

For a moment, Wesley's lips quivered. But then he murmured, "Right. Nothing much."

"You know, Charles," said Patsy, "bottling stuff up all the time can't be good for you. Better to vent off some steam now and then." She whispered a big-sister-to-big-brother aside: "That's especially true for Wesley. He's right . . . well . . . tender, isn't he?"

God's teeth! Patsy was only two years older than he, but she was head-over-heels in love with a neighbor named Henry, a bomber pilot off flying missions over Europe, and she acted like that wartime romance elevated her to an almost adult position. Or at least that's the way it felt to Charles. Still, he admired the way she was always so patient with her younger brothers and Wesley. Charles knew he should try to be more like her, but he hadn't asked to be Wes's nursemaid.

What was it with Americans thinking that talking about feelings helped anything? Charles continued to fume. He'd been completely taken aback by their tendency to hug people they barely knew, and for Virginia ladies to say "Bless your little heart" whenever they met Wesley. Did they really think that talking or hugging or those molasses cookies and lemonade they endlessly offered could wash away the memories of houses shattering, friends trapped under rubble, or ships exploding and burning while survivors clung to wreckage in ten-foot-high waves?

Shut up, Bishop, he cautioned himself. He and Wes had escaped the Nazis' bombs only because of the Ratcliff family's kindness. Their father had saved Mr. Ratcliff's life during World War I, so Mr. Ratcliff had readily agreed to save Wesley and Charles from Hitler's Blitz and London's raging fires. That Ratcliff generosity made him and Wesley among the lucky few—two of only four-thousand-some British child evacuees who'd gotten across the sea safely before Nazi U-boat attacks became so deadly that the British government refused to let more children risk the crossing.

Most of their friends back home still had gas masks hanging around their necks, and hunkered down in underground Tube stations or in flimsy backyard shelters during bombing raids. Charles remembered what it felt like during a Luftwaffe pounding, not knowing what might be left of their life when they crawled back out. He wasn't about to bite the hand that fed him, as the saying went, with some rude demand that Patsy mind her own business.

But he also wasn't about to embarrass himself by opening up. Once, he'd shared some of the realities of the London Blitz with Bobby, the oldest Ratcliff boy and his best friend. Charles had broken down and sobbed bitterly as he did. Bobby had been aces about it, but Charles had been mortified that he'd let someone see him so, well, weak. No, swagger was the better option, the best deflection in such moments.

So as Patsy gently coaxed Wesley—"Was it a bad memory, honey? You can tell me"—Charles swallowed hard, shrugged nonchalantly, and said, "Oh, a few people just took a bit of a dunking."

Wesley's blue eyes seemed to get even bigger and rounder. "It was more than that, Charles. The ship next to us sank so fast, they couldn't get their lifeboats ready in time. Do you suppose any of those people survived?"

Probably not many, Charles thought grimly, but he said with fake cheerfulness, "Oh, I'm sure the follow-up boats got them, Wes. Remember the Royal Navy's orders? Convoys keep moving after a torpedo hit but transmit a distress signal. Our sailors are good lads, the world's best. I bet they had all those people on deck drinking tea within a few hours."

Charles looked at Patsy to gauge her reaction to all this. Her usually friendly and open freckled face looked ashen. "You see . . ." He almost choked on the words; he'd always felt so guilty about leaving those people to the sea's mercy. "With Nazi wolf packs hunting us, slowing down in the middle of an attack to fish people out of the water after their ships were torpedoed was suicidal."

Patsy's eyes welled up. "That's seems . . . so . . . hard-hearted," she whispered.

"That's the war," said Charles. He tried to be matter-of-fact, but he was thrown off his game by the empathy in her large hazel eyes. For one more tantalizing moment, he longed to tell how he'd wondered with terror if he could manage to tread the icy water and hold his little brother up to breathe if their ship went down too. "I . . . It . . ." he began.

But by then the Ratcliff brothers had scrambled out of the water and stood around them in a dripping circle.

"What's the scoop?" asked Bobby. "Something wrong, Chuck?"

Surrounded by boys, Charles automatically switched back to a practiced bravado. He grinned roguishly, his dimples deep, and his blue-gray eyes grew mischievous. "Naaaaw," he said, imitating American slang. "We were just remembering some of the things that happened on our trip across the pond. Like seeing those icebergs, right, Wes?"

"Right, Charles," Wesley answered hesitantly.

"And the whale spouting?"

"Oh yes, that was lovely. I saw its eye!"

"Remember how you children played hide-and-seek amongst the lifeboats piled up on deck?"

"Right!" Wesley began to perk up. "And shuffleboard and tag, and sometimes the crew let us ring the ship's bell."

Charles turned to the Ratcliffs. "There were two hundred kids on board. They ran riot because His Majesty's government could only pay for one adult chaperone per fifteen of them. With so much chaos, we older lads could sneak into the cocktail lounge and drink off the remnants of adult passengers' cocktails."

The Ratcliff boys gasped.

"That's right." Charles had the boys' full attention. "Had my first sip of a martini, dry, olives even." He omitted the fact that it tasted like lighter fluid and he'd spat it out immediately.

"But where were the adults?" asked Bobby.

Charles laughed. "Off throwing up. We had to sail at fifteen knots, in zigzags to make it harder for the Jerries to target us. Everyone was seasick everywhere. We even made up a vomit song. It goes like this." Grinning, he motioned at Wesley to join in.

Wesley took a deep breath and, in his high choir-boy voice, piped out new words to the tune "My Bonnie Lies Over the Ocean":

"My supper went over the ocean,
My breakfast is over the sea,
My tummy is in such an uproar,
Don't bring any dinner to me."

Patsy rolled her eyes.

"EEEEEEWWWW," squealed the twins.

For a brief, wonderful moment, Wesley could tell they admired him. Usually they saw him as far too bookish to look up to.

Bobby slapped Wesley on the back. "Ha-ha-ha, that's the ticket!" he said.

Wesley basked in the boys' approval until Ron—the middle Ratcliff brother—spoke. "Hey, Bobby, you know I tasted moonshine when I was just Jamie and Johnny's age. Me and Tommy skipped school and hung out with some field hands working his daddy's farm. It was . . ."

Bobby ignored his younger brother. "Is a martini as ritzy as the *Phantom Detective* magazine stories say, Chuck?"

Wesley watched Ron's face cloud up as fast as a summer thunderstorm gathered on the river. This time Ron fairly shouted to get Bobby's attention. "Bet Wesley threw up buckets too. Didn't you, old chum?" He said the last two words with a fake British accent and a sneer.

The twins stopped looking impressed and giggled. "Throw up, throw up," they chanted.

Ron was forever going after Wesley. Maybe it was because he and Charles took up space in the Ratcliffs' already crowded farmhouse. Maybe twelve-year-old Ron was jealous of the fact that Bobby seemed to like Charles and Wes so much.

Charles stood, clenching his fists, ready to do battle. Wesley knew his big brother wouldn't stand down either. He'd told Wesley that appeasement never worked with cocky boys like Ron, he'd learned that much at least at his English boys' school. Wesley needed to learn the same, he'd said.

"Boys, boys," Patsy stood as well. "Please, it's such a lovely afternoon."

Neither Ron nor Charles moved. For several seconds, no one spoke, anticipating a punch. There was only the hum of katydids in the trees, until Jamie suddenly started jumping up and down, pointing at the pond. "Hey, y'all! Look! " he shouted. "A water moccasin! Holy mackerel, it's a whopper! Let's get it!"

With so many marshes and creeks coming off the James and York rivers, the Tidewater area was the perfect environment for all sorts of wildlife, including snakes—much to the delight of hawks, herons, and little boys like Johnny and Jamie. One of the first American precautions Wesley had learned, however, was that water moccasins were poisonous.

"Oh no you don't, mister!" Patsy grabbed Jamie before he could jump into the water. Bobby intercepted Johnny, who kicked and screeched in protest.

They watched the greenish-black snake slide in serpentines across the mirror-still water, leaving a trail of S-shaped ripples. At the far bank, it disappeared under a mess of wild roses overhanging the embankment. There was something odd-looking about the shape of the tangled underbrush.

"A TIRE!" they all shouted at the same time.

An old discarded tire had drifted down the creek, gotten caught in the brambles, and stopped, half submerged.

Ker-plunk! Before Patsy could stop them, her brothers dove into the water like bullfrogs. *Kerplunk, kerplunk.* Yanking and shouting, they dragged the frayed tire out of the water.

"Boy oh boy, it's a beaut!" Bobby exclaimed. Since Pearl Harbor, he and Charles had become passionate salvage collectors for the war effort. Bobby pushed his coppery hair out of his eyes so he could look at the tire carefully. "Men," he said. "Oh, and lady." He bowed to his older sister. "This is a treasure trove! Y'all know why?"

"Why?" chirped the twins, clapping their hands.

"Well, I'll tell you. How many old razor blades does it take to make the tail of an air force bomb?"

"A whole twelve thousand," the twins shouted together.

"Right! How many pairs of nylon stockings can make a parachute?"

"I know that one, Mr. General," Patsy said, playing along. "Thirty-six pairs. We collected that many at Girl Scouts."

Bobby nodded. "And it takes five thousand tin cans for a tank shell casing. That's a lot of soup and dog food! But this single, old, beat-up tire, all by its little lonesome, can be recycled into twelve—that's right, folks—twelve gas masks."

"Twelve pilots," breathed Patsy.

"Twelve of our mates back home," Charles said to Wesley.

"Jeepers!" cried the twins.

"Hey! We'll be the first to bring in salvage this year!" crowed Ron. "We'll be heroes!"

Suddenly, school starting the next day was exciting rather than awful.

The Ratcliffs and Bishops trooped home, carrying the tire like a big-animal trophy from a safari hunt. Bobby and Charles led. As they emerged from the woods, they sang a song from a popular Donald Duck cartoon playing in the movie houses. It was full of red-white-and-blue sass and spite, making fun of German oompah-pah bands to ridicule those who'd blindly followed Hitler and his racist beliefs to become Nazis.

"Don't forget to add the raspberry after *Heil*!" called out Bobby.

The boys put their hands under their sweaty armpits and pumped their arms up and down in popping slaps, or stuck their tongues out and blew to make loud farting sounds to replace the Nazi *Seig Heil* salute.

> *"When der fuehrer says we is de master race*
> *We heil* (BLAT), *heil* (BLAT) *right in der fuehrer's face."*

They nearly split their sides with laughing after each fake fart—even Wesley.

12 September 1943

Dear Dad,

I have started 'high school,' as the Yanks call it, and I am back on a team! I jolly well miss cricket but I shall make do with 'football.' By the way, the name itself is daft. Over here they call the real football 'soccer,' and the closest they come is kick-the-can. No, their football is more like rugby, although Americans wear helmets and shoulder pads to play it, Dad! For all their guff about how strong they are, they would never survive our rugger scrums.

Still, I keep that opinion to myself because Bobby is the quarterback, the player who pretty much commands the team. So many seniors left school early to join the service, he recruited me to play tight end. I run wide for passes. Blokes on the other team try to knock me to the ground and hold me there. (Mum would not like it.) But if I catch Bobby's pass and cross the goal line, I am a hero!

Speaking of heroes...May I come home now? The Richmond Times-Dispatch writes that the Blitz has finally quieted a bit and the Yanks have better control over the Atlantic. Cargo ships leave Hampton Roads and Newport News for England almost every day. Fewer are being torpedoed. I wager a captain would take me as a junior crew member. I am ever so much taller since last you saw me—five whole inches. Do not forget, I turn fifteen this spring. I could fight incendiaries with London's fire brigade like you do, Dad. I hate having nipped out when my chums are toughing the war at home.

I do not mean to complain. Mr and Mrs Ratcliff are very kind, and we do have a good laugh with the brothers. This weekend, we raced wheelbarrows down the farm's lane. I put Wes in mine and Bobby put the twins in his. Ron was the flagman to start us. You will not believe what happened! The lane is shaded by walnut trees, and a black snake fell off the branches, smack-dab onto Wes! It had been lurking up there waiting for some unsuspecting squirrel. A doozy of a serpent—six feet long! Nothing like it in England except maybe Nessie. But the brothers turned it loose because it keeps mice out of the crops.

Of course, Wesley set off blubbering about it. Honestly, he does go on. Do you know he still stows Joey under his pillow? If the brothers find him with a stuffed koala bear, he will catch all manner of grief. They are good hearts, but a tough lot, farming and all, you know.

Yours, Charles

Chapter Two

"There!" Charles stuck a red thumbtack into Sicily. He took a step back from the world map he'd hung on their bedroom wall to admire his trail of pins. "Now we're talking."

Wesley stopped fanning himself with a *Superman* comic book. The brothers shared an attic room under the gabled eaves of the Ratcliffs' green tin roof. Even though the white clapboard farmhouse was shaded by oak trees, they sweltered in warm months. That September afternoon the temperature had spiked back up to ninety, and their rotating circular fan only did so much good. But it was the only place for them in the three-bedroom house. The four American brothers were crammed together in one big bedroom on the second floor. Patsy, being the only girl, was given a small room to herself, and their parents occupied the last one.

Wesley tossed the comic book and stood to look at the map more closely. "We're doing better now, aren't we, Charles?"

"Quite!" Charles grinned at him. He pointed at the black-and-white photograph of Winston Churchill he'd pasted on the sloping ceiling. In it, Churchill made his famous V for Victory sign. "The Prime Minister showed us how to stand tall, all right. Remember what he said after Dunkirk, when France fell and we ended up facing Hitler all by ourselves?" Charles lowered his voice to a growl: "'We shall not flag or fail. . . .'"

Wes joined him: "'We shall defend our island, whatever the cost may be. . . . We shall never surrender!'"

"Well done!" Charles applauded Wesley's recitation. He turned back to Churchill's image. "Now that we Allies have taken Sicily and landed at Salerno, we've got Hitler's Italian pals out of the fight at least. Maybe within the year, we can move up the boot of Italy and push the Nazis back over the Alps!" Jokingly, Charles saluted Churchill's round, jowly face.

In their bedroom, Charles tended to drop the American persona he was trying so hard to perfect and be unabashedly British with Wesley. He'd hung up a Union Jack flag, models of RAF Spitfires, and photos of their parents, plus the king and prime minister. Over Charles's bed was a picture of his school cricket team. Their father, a geography teacher, coached it.

Instinctively imitating his father's teaching specialty, Charles had been tracking the progress of the Allied armies on his large map. He'd agonized over British defeats—retreats from Greece, Crete, and island after island in Southeast Asia. Finally, that spring, the tide had turned, starting in North Africa with the defeat of Rommel, Hitler's "Desert Fox" tank commander.

Charles continued, more to himself than to Wesley: "*If*

the Russians can survive Hitler's siege of Leningrad, and *if* the Americans can finally invade France, and *if* the Allies can take all of Italy, we should be able to squeeze Nazi Germany from three sides." He put his hands on his hips and cocked his head, looking at his maps like an army general planning a campaign. "The operating word here is *if* we can do all those things," Charles muttered.

It wasn't looking so great in Russia, for instance. The Nazis had blockaded Leningrad for more than three years. And nobody knew when the Allies would attempt a land invasion of occupied France. American and British pilots were flying near-suicide missions over Europe to bomb Nazi ammunition factories to "loosen things up" before a beach landing of ground troops could be dared. The air forces were losing planes right and left. Patsy's sweetheart, Henry, had written that flyers averaged only fifteen missions before their planes were shot down.

It was beginning to feel like the war would go on forever, that evacuating "for the duration" meant he and Wesley might be permanently stranded in the States. He wasn't sure he could stand that. Even though he and Bobby were good mates and he was enjoying high school, Charles was antsy to return to England and do his part. Several of his old school chums had become nighttime air raid wardens. Charles feared some of them called him a coward for evacuating to the U.S.

He reached over to the dresser he shared with Wesley to pick up his souvenir lump of shrapnel. He tossed it back and forth between his hands like a ball as he mulled things over. Back home, after air raids, he and his mates had emerged from their backyard Anderson shelters and searched for smoldering bits of flak from London's antiaircraft cannon. Charles even had a shard of a Nazi warplane, a knife-sized piece of red metal—probably part of the Nazi Iron Cross painted on Luftwaffe planes. He'd found it down the street from his house after a horrible night of bombs and fires, a tiny remnant of one of the few Nazi raiders the London ack-ack antiaircraft guns had stopped.

For a moment his mind flew home, wondering what his street looked like now. He tried to walk it in his memory, replanting all the rosebushes that had been charred, rebricking the fences that had tumbled down, to make the lane peaceful again. Charles felt his throat tighten and shook his head to rid himself of the image of destruction.

"Yes, a big *if*," he repeated, going back to his analysis of Allied strategy of trying to surround Hitler's strongholds. "Unlike the Yanks, we know firsthand how big a fight the Nazis will put up, don't we, Wes," he murmured.

"What did you say, Charles?"

Charles turned away from the map to look at his brother, about to repeat his worries loudly enough for Wesley to hear. But he stopped himself. Wesley's mop of blond curls and peaches-and-cream complexion gave him a typical British appearance but also emphasized how young he was, reminding Charles that as much as he needed to talk out his concerns, his younger brother wasn't emotionally ready to hear Charles's worries that the Allies might fail.

"Oh, nothing." Charles put the blackened lump down. "Say, don't you have lessons to learn?"

Wesley sighed. "Yes. I have to memorize the forty-eight states and their capitals, although it won't be much use when I get home. I worry about not knowing my British geography."

"I know," said Charles. "I should have finished translating Virgil by now, and this high school doesn't even offer Latin. Their one teacher of it is off with the navy. How the deuce does Dad expect me to win entrance to Cambridge?"

He gestured for Wesley's homework. "Here, want me to test you?"

"Really? You don't mind?"

"Not at all. The only reading I have is for English Literature and I've already studied all the books on the syllabus."

"Smashing!" Wesley handed Charles a list he'd written out for homework. "See how far I can recite. I need to spell them correctly, too."

"Right-o." Charles stretched out on his bed in the stream of the fan.

"Alabama, Montgomery. A-l-a-b-a-m-a, M-o-n-t-g-o-m-e-r-y."

Charles nodded, thinking back on the capitals he'd had to memorize at Wesley's age—Bombay, Nairobi, Johannesburg—places that were part of the British Empire.

"Kentucky, Frankfort," Wesley was continuing. "F-r-a-n-k-f-o-r-t."

"F-*u*-r-t," Charles interrupted.

"No, Charles, it's not like the German city. It's *o*-r-t."

"Rubbish."

"No, truly."

"He's right, Chuck," Bobby had climbed the stairs without Charles hearing him over the rattle and whirl of the fan and was leaning against the doorway. He grinned at Wesley. "I didn't realize you were so good at spelling, Wes. You know what? You should enter the county spelling bee. Bet dollars to doughnuts you'd win. Patsy won it when she was your age. I tried to keep up the tradition, but failed miserably!" He laughed. "And we can't count on Ron to keep up the family tradition either. He's my brother and I'd clobber anyone else who said this, but sometimes I think Ron was standing behind the barn door when they handed out brains—for schoolwork anyway. So, you need to enter it for us. We'd be mighty proud if you brought that trophy home again."

"Gee, thanks, Bobby."

Wesley beamed.

Charles had watched Bobby have that effect on countless boys, especially on the football team. Bobby had a confident friendliness and an ease with giving out compliments that, generally speaking, Brits didn't. Charles had come to really appreciate that about some Americans. He'd also marveled at the fact Bobby didn't seem to mind that he and Wesley occupied the attic room which Bobby could have claimed for himself as the eldest Ratcliff brother. Charles would try to replicate that kind of instinctive generosity when he got home to England.

"Came to tell you the bathroom's yours now, Chuck," said Bobby. "Then I need your help candling today's eggs to check for bloodspots before crating them, okay? We've got a passel to deal with. The hens are in fine form."

"Shore 'nough," Charles answered in an exaggerated Virginia drawl as he grabbed his towel.

Laughing, Bobby and Charles bounded down the stairs together.

12 September 1943

Dearest Mummy,

How is Hamlet? Are you able to spare him a soup bone these days? I wish I could send some of our food. Nothing posh, but quite tasty. Pancakes with maple syrup are smashing!

The new school term has started. It is perfectly AWFUL. I have been skipped ahead to seventh grade because of being 'so advanced.' Everyone is almost two years older and so much BIGGER. The worst is Ron is in my class because he had to repeat the grade! Our teacher, Miss Darling, thinks because he brought in an old tire for salvage that Ron is some natural-born leader. She put him in charge of our class's war efforts. It has quite gone to his head. He bullied one poor chap into stealing his mother's girdle to bring in for our rubber collection!

Even worse is studying the American Revolution. Was King George III really such a tyrant? It is quite hard being British when the teacher goes on about the Boston 'massacre' and 'lobsterbacks' gunning down a crowd of 'innocents.' Now Ron has got everyone calling me 'the Tory.'

I wish Charles were around at recess. But he has entered high school and larks about with older boys and tries to sound American. He even calls himself "Chuck."

The heat is BEASTLY. It is hard to breathe until nighttime during American summers. But then fireflies light up in the grass. Have I told you about fireflies? They twinkle! They drift through the air to the trees and light them up in flashes through the night. We catch them and they crawl about, blinking on our fingertips. Sometimes I pretend I have caught little shooting stars.

But there are also terrifying things here too, Mummy. The other day an ENORMOUS snake fell out of a tree right on me. It tried to wrap itself around my throat, just like Kaa in The Jungle Book. If Charles had not pulled it off, I might be D-E-A-D now.

I miss you ever so much, and things like the sound of London's church bells. Does Big Ben still chime the hour despite being scorched by the Luftwaffe? Have you got our roof built back where it shattered from old Adolf's bombs dropping on the street?

I try not to worry, but I haven't heard from you for FIVE WHOLE WEEKS. Your last patch of letters must have been sunk by the Jerries. Do let me know you are all right.

Your loving son,
Wesley Bishop

Chapter Three

Wesley settled back in to study until Charles got out of the shower. Then he'd try to nab the bathroom himself. He'd have to move quickly. With nine people, the one bathroom was in constant use. And on a hot, dry day, everyone wanted to spritz off. Of course, showers in general were still a treat to Wesley. Like most British homes, their ancient London row house had only a bathtub.

Wesley forced himself to stop imagining a refreshing shower. He went back to his list. "North Dakota, Bismarck." He stopped. "Dakota" was an Indian name, just like the Chickahominy River nearby. "What an odd thing to have a state named for Indians and its capital named for a German province." *The Bismarck* also happened to be the name of a notorious Nazi battleship that had shelled cargo ships crossing the Atlantic.

"Boy, if I lived in Bismarck," Wesley muttered to himself, "I'd change that name for sure. To something like . . ." His eyes searched the room for an idea and landed on the day's newspaper funnies. "Tonto!" He struck on the name of the loyal Indian guide in the comic strip and on his favorite radio program, *The Lone Ranger*. "Yes! Tonto!"

Bored with studying, Wesley got up and stretched. With one arm up, like the Ranger when he waved his cowboy hat in good-bye, Wesley laughed and echoed the character's departing line as he rode away on his white horse: "Hi-ho, Silver, away!"

He shook his head. Given Hollywood movies, he'd completely expected to see cowboys and Indians everywhere when he came to the States. Wesley had been so disappointed not to meet any on the streets of Richmond, the Ratcliffs had given him toy six-shooters and a holster for his first American Christmas.

Wesley looked back over his shoulder to make sure he was alone. Then he slowly opened the drawer of the desk he and Charles used. He'd recently stashed the present there, telling himself he was too old for imaginary games. Oh, but he'd had such fun pretending with those guns.

Hesitantly, fondly, he pulled them out. Enough geography for the moment, he told himself. No one's looking. Wesley strapped on the holster. Facing the window, his back to the door, he held his hands out parallel to his six-shooters, like a sheriff in a Wild West showdown getting ready to fire at some low-down, good-for-nothing gunslinger. Wesley took a few slow steps imagining the sound of spurs jingling as he moved. He snarled, "Git out of my town, you two-bit outlaw, before I string ya up."

He smiled ruefully and was about to take the guns off and tuck them back in the drawer, when he heard: "What a baby! You still play make-believe?"

Wesley wheeled around. Ron was at the door.

"Wait till I tell the class. They'll laugh you out of school, straight back to that stupid little island of yours. 'Pip-pip, cheerio, and all that rot.'"

Wesley's fingers twitched beside his play six-shooters. For a moment, he wished they were real. Bet Ron wouldn't pick on him then! Why was it that he could never come up with a proper retort for Ron? Charles always did.

Ron entered the room and circled him. "Cat got your tongue?" Ron glanced back at the door, clearly timing his bullying to end before Charles came back. Then he spotted Wesley's state capital list. "You did that already?" It wasn't due until the end of the week. He snatched it up.

"That's mine," Wesley protested.

"Now it's mine." Ron folded it and stuffed it into the chest pocket of his overalls.

"Give that back!"

"Come and get it, runt."

Wesley knew he'd never win a wrestling match with Ron. He also knew what Ron was going to do with that paper—he'd turn it in for homework as if he'd done it himself. "That's cheating," he cried.

"What you gonna do? Tell the teacher?" Ron closed in on Wesley and towered over him. Ron was lean and muscular, tall for his age, like Bobby was. But his hair was darker than his sibling's, a bloodred almost, and his face typically carried a brooding scowl that made him slightly sinister in Wesley's eyes.

Wesley had quickly learned that tattling was a cardinal sin among American boys. If Wesley ran to the teacher or Charles or Bobby for help, it'd only make Ron see him as a total weakling. And that would encourage Ron to torture him more. "Fine," Wesley squeaked. "I already know them all. It will only take me a few minutes to rewrite it. Have it."

Then, as Ron stepped back with a smirk on his face, Wesley did think of a comeback. It so surprised him, it came out only as a whisper: "Of course, the real trick for you, Ron, will be trying to *learn* and actually remember forty-eight states and capitals."

Ron heard. His face turned as red as the tomatoes the Ratcliffs raised and sold to the Piggly Wiggly grocery store. He grabbed Wesley's arm. "You calling me stupid?"

No more clever retorts came to Wesley. He wondered how much a bloody nose would hurt.

But just as Ron was pulling his other hand back to punch Wesley, Charles entered the room, rubbing his hair with a towel.

Ron let go. He took a step back as Charles pulled the terry cloth off his head and noticed the two boys standing there.

"What's going on?" Charles demanded. "What are you doing up here, Ron?"

Wesley could see that Charles was immediately suspicious of Ron. Their last fight—over shoes—had been awful. Since leather was needed for army equipment, new shoes for civilians were rationed. The younger boys made do with the older boys' cast-offs. When Mrs. Ratcliff saw that Wesley's feet were bloody with blisters because of how tight his old shoes were, she made Ron give Wesley his favorite Converse All Stars, even though they weren't quite too small for him yet. Ron was so mad about it he went after Wesley but ended up punching Charles in the face, when Charles told him to back off. Things only got more tense when Mr. Ratcliff gave Ron a tanning after learning why Charles had a split lip.

Perhaps remembering that episode, Ron played innocent. "Mama sent me to get Wesley," he said. "Because the Japs captured the East Indies we can't get kapok to stuff life preservers with anymore. So there's a call for milkweed pods. They say a pound and a half of milkweed floss will keep a one-hundred-fifty-pound sailor afloat for ten hours."

"Get out of town! For real?" Bobby was now in the doorway too. "That weed we're always trying to pull out of the cornfield can save a man's life?"

"Yeah," Ron answered. "Good old *American* ingenuity figured that out."

As if the British couldn't have seen that, thought Wesley.

Ron continued, "Here's the best news: the factory making life preservers will pay fifteen cents for each cotton sack of pods. So Mama said me and Wesley could skip our regular chores to collect pods."

"Fifteen whole cents per bag?" repeated Bobby. He whistled. "There must be a ton of that stuff growing along our fence line—a dollar's worth for sure, maybe even five!"

Wesley sure didn't like the idea of spending the afternoon

with Ron. But he did like the idea of contributing some money to the mason jar of change in the kitchen. The Depression had sucked away most all Mr. Ratcliff's savings, and Wesley and Charles were painfully aware that the money their parents sent didn't equal what it cost the Ratcliffs to feed and clothe them.

Wesley knew Charles would go pick pods even if faced with a dozen bullies. He looked up at the photo of Churchill and steeled himself. "All righty, then," he said, and picked up the straw hat he wore to shade his fair-skinned face while picking vegetables.

"Watch your back," Charles warned as Wesley passed him.

Chapter Four

Ron and Wesley walked the edge of the Ratcliff farm, picking pods off the chest-high milkweeds. In June, the plants' fragrant purple flowers hummed with bees. In August, their lush leaves crawled with black-and-gold-striped caterpillars that morphed into monarch butterflies. Now, in September, the stalks were dried and fragile, seemingly lifeless. But each held up pods as big as chicken drumsticks, crammed full with life to come—wispy dandelion-like tufts that would carry seeds on the winds once the pods cracked open enough to release them.

During Wesley's first autumn in Virginia, milkweed had been a terrific game with Patsy. "Never say there's no fun to be had on a farm," she'd told the two Londoners. She took all the boys out into the fields and pulled the pods apart to send the seeds floating. The brothers ran underneath blowing in puffs to see who could keep their seed off the ground the longest. Jamie and Johnny had tumbled all over each other as they followed the drifting seeds.

Wesley stopped snapping off pods for a moment and watched the twins, who had come along with him and Ron. Instead of helping to pick pods they were playing "red light, green light." Wesley couldn't help feeling jealous of their being able to play while he labored. He straightened the shoulder strap of his cotton-picking sack with some irritation. His bag was getting full and clumsy to drag. But it wasn't heavy. The milkweed fluff was that lightweight.

"Green light!"

The twins dashed past him, their strawberry blond hair dancing. Jamie pulled ahead of Johnny and ran up behind Ron, slapping his butt to claim his big brother as home base. "Safe!" Jamie shouted.

"Hey! Watch it!" Ron pushed Jamie off him. "Take a hike!" He turned back to his picking.

"I won! I won!" Jamie crowed.

"You cheated!" Johnny cried, panting as he caught up. "You took off before we said 'green light!'"

"Did not!"

"Did too!"

"You're just a sore loser," Jamie shouted.

"Am not!"

"Are too!"

Wesley knew it was a matter of seconds before the first shove. As predictable as the twins' tussles were, there was still something entertaining about them. They never truly hurt each other. When they really got into it, rolling around and swatting at each other, they looked like one of those blurred images in Looney Tunes cartoon fights, where there was a whirling ball of fists with *X*s and *oof*s flying out of it.

There it was—Johnny pushed Jamie hard. Jamie staggered, then shoved back. Reeling, Johnny took a few forward steps for momentum and really shouldered Jamie. Johnny's counterattack sent Jamie flying—right into Ron. All three of them landed on the ground with a loud thump and squeals of pain.

Johnny and Jamie lay there, gasping and whining and giggling all at the same time, still slapping at each other good-naturedly.

It was clear, however, that Ron was not amused. The weight of the three of them had smashed his sack of milkweed. Just like a pillow might split during a pillow fight to send feathers flying, Ron's milkweed pods had exploded into a cloud of wisps that drifted away.

Ron exploded as well. "Just wait until I get my hands on you dopes!" He grabbed for his little brothers. They wormed away in swift, practiced dodges and got to their feet to run.

Wesley knew they wouldn't get far before Ron, who was twice their size, would catch them.

Shrieking, the twins darted straight for Wesley. They wrapped their arms around his waist and cowered behind him. "Save us!" they yelled.

Wesley was stunned. They were still playing a game, he

knew. But even so, the twins had never before turned to him for help. He looked down at them in surprise, then up at Ron coming toward him. *Blimey!* Now I'll catch it, he thought.

But Ron stopped. His mouth popped open. His look of rage turned to one of surprise, and—Wesley couldn't be entirely sure, but it looked like Ron's feelings were hurt. His brow puckered as he looked at his brothers, the same expression Wesley had seen on Ron's face when Bobby went off on some lark with Charles.

Then Ron crossed his arms over his chest, and that chip-on-his-shoulder look that always meant trouble for Wesley settled onto his face. "Turncoats." He spit out the word.

Jamie and Johnny peeped out from behind Wesley. "What did you call us?"

"Turncoats," he barked.

"What does that mean?" they chimed.

"Someone who chooses the enemy over family. Someone who switches sides to save his own skin."

The twins let go of Wesley. "We're not no turncoats," Johnny whimpered.

"Prove it," Ron challenged.

Jamie and Johnny came to attention like little soldiers.

Ron pointed at the fluff floating away on the air. "See that? You wrecked my work. That's about five American sailors who won't have a Mae West to keep them alive now, thanks to you two knuckleheads. They'll drown instead."

The twins glanced at each other in horror as if caught committing a terrible crime.

Ron peeled off his cotton sack and tossed it at them. "Fill

this back up to prove you're behind me and that you back the U.S. of A."

"Okay, Ron. We will!" The twins took up the cotton sack. Dragging it between them, they took turns standing on tiptoe to pluck the pods. As carefree as they'd been earlier, they were now filled with patriotic purpose.

Pretty clever the way Ron got the twins to do his work for him. Wesley stewed as he continued to fill his own sack. Then he noticed Johnny wiping his face with his shirtsleeves. He was crying.

"That was mean, Ron." The words came out of Wesley's mouth before he could stop the thought. He even dared to repeat it. "Making the twins feel like they were turncoats for hiding behind me and that they didn't care about American sailors was plain old mean."

Ron glared at Wesley, and called ahead, "Hey, boys, do you know when Americans started using the word 'turncoat'?"

"When, Ron?" Jamie spoke for the two of them. Johnny was still sniffling.

"During the Revolutionary War. When we had to fight the . . ."—he paused for emphasis—"British."

Living not far from Williamsburg and Yorktown, where the Americans finally beat the British, the twins knew a good amount about the Revolutionary War, despite being just second graders. They stopped picking to listen.

"Yup, the British," Ron went on, reciting the history their teacher had just covered the day before. "Like old Wesley here. Taxation without representation, don't you know. The Brits tried to take our freedom. They would have hanged George Washington and Thomas Jefferson if they'd gotten their hands on them."

The twins frowned and glanced at Wesley suspiciously. Washington and Jefferson were like gods in Virginia. Ron was on a roll.

"There were even some turncoats right here in Virginia." Ron pointed east, where just a few miles down the road enormous old plantation houses built in the 1700s still stood along the riverbanks. "When the British fleet sailed up and down the James lobbing cannonballs at people's farms, some planters who'd claimed to be patriots turned into loyalists when they thought being loyal to the king was safer."

"What happened to turncoats?" Jamie asked.

"Well, I'll tell you, Jamie." Ron put his arm across his little brother's shoulders. "When patriots realized they had British sympathizers in town, they'd haul them into the street and tar and feather them." He looked toward Wesley and cocked his head, as if imagining Wesley covered in white chicken feathers.

Jamie and Johnny followed his lead.

Wesley held his breath to see what Ron would say next. Bobby might think Ron had no brains, but this speech of his was diabolically clever.

"But aren't we friends with the British now?" Johnny asked.

"Of course we are. And us Americans are good friends, too. Hitler would have starved out the Brits if it hadn't been for us sending ships with American food and American fuel and American parts for their trucks and airplanes. Think about all those ships sailing out of Norfolk and Hampton Roads for

England, braving the high seas and Nazi submarines. Remember those tankers of ours being blown to smithereens right off Virginia Beach?"

The twins nodded. Wesley remembered too. One of the Ratcliff neighbors was enjoying a day of sunbathing when she witnessed four ships explode and burn from mines a Nazi U-boat had managed to string at the mouth of the harbor. After the girl recounted the scene, Wesley had had to rush outside to throw up in the bushes.

Ron continued: "But we didn't stop sailing, did we? Even with those dirty rotten Nazi subs waiting off Virginia's coast to blow up our ships? Our ships keep going out."

The twins shook their heads. "No, not us. We don't stop."

"Some people even say the only reason the Japanese attacked Pearl Harbor was because we'd stuck out our necks for the Brits . . . again . . . just like in World War I. But"—Ron shrugged—"that's what friends do, right? Otherwise the great British Empire might be just another Krautville right now."

Wesley's face flamed with fury at the insinuation the British were weak charity cases. But before he could manage any kind of reply, Ron changed the subject. "Say, you boys did a great job. The bag's full again. How about a swim? It's hot."

"Gee, thanks, Ron!" chorused the twins.

Ron smiled down at them as sweet as honey. He turned to Wesley. "Coming, old chum?"

Smarting from Ron's not-so-concealed insults, Wesley wasn't interested in getting himself into a situation that facilitated further harassment. "No thanks," he managed to answer.

"I'm going to fill another sack. Your mum can use the fifteen cents to buy a quart of milk."

Ron narrowed his eyes. "Trying to show me up?" he said in a lowered voice only Wesley could hear. "No way." Then he announced loudly, "It's hot. We all deserve a break. You too, Wesley. You don't want us to feel guilty if we go on to the pond and you stay here, do you? You'd spoil it for the twins."

"Yeah, don't be a spoilsport," said Jamie.

That was that.

As soon as they reached the pool's clearing, the Ratcliff boys stripped down to their boxers. They dove in, scrambled out, and dove in again—over and over. Wesley floated along the opposite bank.

"Hey, y'all, who do I remind you of?" Ron stood at the water's edge, thumped his chest, and bellowed: "AAAAHH-a-a-a-AAAAAAHHH-a-a-a."

"Tarzan!" squealed the twins in delight.

Hearing them, even Wesley laughed. He had to admit Ron's imitation was spot-on. The yodeling scream was the hallmark of the films, including the one they'd just seen—*Tarzan Triumphs*—in which Tarzan battled Nazis who'd come to the jungle and captured Boy. Ron gripped a thick grapevine hanging off a willow oak and swung himself over the water, just like Tarzan swung from tree to tree. Ron let go at just the right moment to drop—SPLASH!—into the water.

"Oh-oh-oh! I want to do it!" the twins chanted. Ron helped them hold the grapevine and pushed them out over the water.

SPLASH! SPLASH!

They came up spluttering and giggling, just as Ron cannonballed into the water. The Ratcliff brothers' laughter pealed through the woods. Wesley knew Charles would have been right in the middle of that happy roughhousing. He was so tired of feeling like an outsider.

Determined to be a part of the fun for once, he climbed out of the water. As Ron helped the twins onto his grapevine again, Wesley grabbed the vine nearest him. He had to tug hard to get its tentacle hairs to pull free of the tree trunk. He gripped the vine tight, walked backward, and then leaped onto it, wrapping his legs around it tight to clasp it close to his body.

He swung over the water, triumphant that he had managed such an athletic move, and let out his own Tarzan scream. As Wesley slid down the stubbly vine to drop into the water he could see the surprised look on the brothers' faces.

SPLASH!

He surfaced and bobbed, grinning at the boys treading water in his wake. He waited for their congratulations, their pulling him into their raucous circle.

Jamie and Johnny looked horrified. Ron? This time Wesley couldn't decipher his expression.

"What's wrong?" Wesley asked.

Together, Jamie and Johnny pointed to his vine and recited: "Only a dope swings on a hairy rope."

Within two days, Wesley was covered head to toe with poison ivy.

Chapter Five

Wesley put down his pencil and scratched. Patsy had helped him coat his poison ivy rash with pink calamine lotion. It did ease the burning itch, although the dried blobs of candy-colored lotion made him look like a teatime pastry. It was bad enough going to school, but he'd be laughed off the stage if he had to go to the countywide spelling bee looking like this.

He glanced self-consciously at his classmates, who still labored over a test on the Declaration of Independence. He knew they called him a know-it-all. And many of them had delighted in repeating the twins' rhymed warning about poison ivy emphasizing the word "dope." But maybe he could win some friends if he won the county contest as the school's representative.

Wesley had snagged his school's championship on the word "connoisseur." The girl he was up against didn't realize English words could have French spellings. But Wesley had to admit he'd also been lucky. He'd nearly washed out in the very first go-round! Thank goodness he'd remembered that Americans pronounced "been" like trash "bin," rather than the proper British way of saying "been" with long *e*'s, like "bean."

Folding his hands to keep himself from scratching more, Wesley waited for the other students to catch up. He stared at the war posters behind Miss Darling's desk to pass the time. In one, a sailor carrying his gear glanced back over his shoulder, smiling confidently. But across the poster shouted the warning: IF YOU TELL WHERE HE'S GOING . . . HE MAY NEVER GET THERE!

Each morning, Miss Darling patted that sailor's butt before sitting at her desk. Petite and baby-doll pretty, with painted red fingernails and matching lipstick, she'd been pulled out of Mary Washington College early to teach because so many experienced teachers had been called up for service. Sometimes she came to school with absolutely no lesson plan. But her beau was a swabbie, trained at the Norfolk Naval Base and recently shipped out for duty, so the students excused her disorganization, especially the girls, who idolized her for the aura of tragic young love that hung about her.

She'd cried as she described saying good-bye outside the Hampton Roads docks, surrounded by hundreds of women embracing their men, perhaps for the last time. "I can't tell y'all more," she'd whimpered as she blew her nose. "Loose lips sink ships, you know." So whenever Miss Darling gazed out the window, leaned her dimpled face against her hand, and let out long, sad sighs, the class patiently doodled or passed notes.

She was doing it again now. A few of the boys were taking advantage to compare test answers—including Ron.

Wesley squirmed and shifted his focus to a far scarier poster. This one was taped just above the large bucket of sand each classroom had to douse fires in case bombs were dropped on the schoolhouse. Its bold-type headline read: BITS OF CARELESS TALK ARE PIECED TOGETHER BY THE ENEMY. Under that, a huge hand wearing a Nazi swastika ring put together a jigsaw puzzle with the words: CONVOY SAILS FOR ______ TONIGHT. The hand gripped a piece with the word ENGLAND.

Wesley swallowed hard. The posters carried a lot of weight for him. And should for all his classmates, he thought, given where they lived. Tidewater Virginia had become one of the busiest areas in the country in terms of the war effort. Richmond factories made parachutes, flak jackets, bomb clusters, and oxygen masks. Due east down the James River, Norfolk was the main training hub for the U.S. Navy; Newport News produced warships as fast as possible; and Hampton Roads was a major embarkation point for U.S. servicemen leaving to fight in the Atlantic, North Africa, and Europe.

Morning to night, Wesley heard the distant whistles of trains carrying food, medical supplies, ammunition, and equipment into nearby Bellwood, the army's main supply depot on the East Coast. The cargo was soon sent on to Hampton Roads and lowered into the hulls of freighters that steamed out the Chesapeake Bay to the Atlantic, most bound—as the poster said—for England. For home.

But just beyond the mouth of the Chesapeake Bay, half submerged in the waves, waiting, watching, could be Nazi U-boats.

In the months following Pearl Harbor, Hitler's submarines had easily spotted American cargo ships silhouetted against the bright city lights of the American East Coast. Ron had been right about how many had been sunk. It'd been like shooting fish in a barrel for the Nazis, until the United States finally wised up and enforced nighttime blackouts.

The poster made Wesley nervous. He closed his eyes against it. But his mind filled with an incident from that morning, as he, Charles, and the brothers dawdled along Route 5 on the way to school, picking up stray apples that had fallen to the ground from roadside trees. Suddenly Charles had frozen. "What the deuce! Hear that?"

The other boys stopped. The faint sounds of a song reached them.

"Die Fahne hoch! Die Reihen fest geschlossen!"

"Is that German?" Bobby asked.

"Yes." Charles's voice was sharp. "That's a Nazi song. Who would be stupid enough..."

Grinding gears and the roar of huge motors interrupted him. Around the bend came a line of six-wheeled army trucks. Their flatbeds were crammed full of soldiers—German soldiers.

"Bloody hell," breathed Charles. He raised his arm to hurl the hard apples at them as the first truck blew past—Wesley recognized his big brother's killer cricket pitch windup.

Bobby grabbed Charles's wrist. "Hold up, Chuck. They're POWs. They've surrendered. We have to treat them with respect. We want the Third Reich to do the same for our boys."

"Like the respect they gave me and my family before smashing London with their bombs?" Charles tried to push Bobby off. "Let go of me!"

"You're going to have to get used to them being around, Chuck," Bobby said. He didn't let go. "Listen to me. I heard about this at school. They'll be shipped in through Hampton Roads in big numbers, now that we've won in North Africa. They're putting twelve hundred of them at Bellwood to do rail line repairs, laundry, and kitchen duties. A couple thousand more will be held at Camp Lee."

"Are you kidding me?" Charles cried. "We'll be surrounded by Jerries!"

Three more trucks passed by, peppering them with dust. Charles wrenched his arm away from Bobby and shielded his eyes so he could see. "They're still in uniform!" he gasped.

Wesley squinted and peered too. As another truck passed, he could make out the dreaded Nazi eagle on their caps and breast pockets. The soldiers looked well fed and clean. Wesley couldn't believe it. They didn't seem scared or broken or like they were prisoners in a foreign, hostile land. They kept singing:

"Marschier'n im Geist in unser'n Reihen mit!"

"Shut your gob!" Charles screamed. "Shut it!"

One of the Germans smiled and waved back.

Wesley's eyes popped back open. The memory made his already itchy skin crawl.

What if one of those POWs escaped and got information about Bellwood's depot to the U-boats that still trolled along the North Carolina and Virginia shoreline? Hitler might just order the Luftwaffe to bomb Richmond. Or maybe he'd send in saboteurs. Hadn't they caught four Nazi bomb experts in Florida, put ashore by a U-boat life raft, carrying fuses disguised as pencils and $174,000 in American money?

If the Nazis bombed Richmond like they'd bombed London, no supplies—no food, no fuel, no medicines—would be leaving Virginia's ports. How would England survive without those supplies? How would his parents?

Feeling panicky, Wesley reached into his pants pocket to make sure he had the handkerchief all U.S. children were supposed to bring to school to stuff into their mouths to protect their teeth in case of a bomb blast. He'd forgotten it, of course.

Wesley ransacked his shirt pocket for a scrap of reassurance he'd just started carrying. He pulled out a small, tightly folded piece of paper.

Wesley's frantic checking of his pockets drew Ron's attention. "Hey, Miss Darling," he called, and pointed. "Wesley is cheating!"

Desks squeaked as twenty children swung around to look at him. Wesley froze, paper in hand.

Miss Darling turned from the window to the classroom. She seemed confused.

"Look, Miss Darling," Ron pressed. "He has a cheat sheet."

The students' heads swung back to Miss Darling to see what she would do. Slowly, she stood. "Wesley," she said in a quavering voice, almost like she had been caught doing something wrong herself. "I... I expected more from you. What do you have to say for yourself?"

Heads swung back to Wesley.

His mouth popped open. But no words came out.

Miss Darling frowned. Hushed, the class waited as she seemed to search for what to do next. The classroom clock ticked loudly. The sound of a teacher walking in heels echoed down the hall, *tap-tap-tap-tap*. Wesley's heartbeat pounded in his head.

Finally, Miss Darling spoke in an old-lady voice, "Young man, I must ask you to read that piece of paper to the class."

Wesley shook his head.

"Would you prefer a trip to the principal?"

Back home a trip to the headmaster typically meant a caning on a student's backside. So, no, he wouldn't prefer a trip to the principal, reasoned Wesley. Trembling with embarrassment, he opened the precious paper. The class leaned toward him as he choked out: "*Both well, safe. Letters on way. Chin up. Love.*"

It was a telegram from his parents—a standard form the British allowed to be sent to child evacuees in the United States. Wesley's parents had cabled it to answer his worry about not having received any letters from home for so long. A telegram that told Wesley that at least on the day it was sent, his parents were alive and unharmed.

"It's from my mum and dad," he murmured, without looking up from the paper.

Miss Darling covered her mouth with both hands. Then she dashed down the row of desks to grab him up in a hug. "Bless your little heart!" She burst into tears. All the girls looked like they might cry too.

She scrambled to make amends. "Do your parents know about your winning our spelling bee and going to county? I know they'd be bursting their coat buttons they'd be so proud of you, honeybunch. Just like we all are."

The girls nodded. The boys looked like they might throw up.

"Let's forget about this bad old test," she crooned. "Everyone gets a one hundred. I'm calling an early recess. Everyone outside, it's a beeeeea-U-ti-ful day. Shoo. G'on now!"

Cheering, the class scattered. A few even patted Wesley on the back in thanks before darting after their friends.

"Except," Miss Darling called out loudly, as she aimed her pointer finger at Ron. "Except for you, Ronald Ratcliff. You stay behind, please."

4 October 1943

Dear Dad,

Going to school with girls is absolutely top-notch! I swear American high school girls are almost all as pretty as Rita Hayworth. But it is hard to concentrate in class sometimes when they wear perfume. Is that why we Brits split into boy schools and girl schools? It does make for us not understanding one another very well, though, I must say. Sometimes I humiliate myself around Patsy because I am so used to shooting the breeze with other chaps. And then, of course, with Wesley being so young, she lumps us both into a kid category, which is quite irksome and makes me bungle things even worse with her.

I am trying to help Wes toughen up a bit and not be quite so homesick. The middle Ratcliff boy, Ron, razzes him all the time.

A big game called homecoming is this Friday night. It will be perfect carnival with a bonfire, the marching band playing in a "pep rally," and cheerleaders jumping up and down leading chants. Homecoming means graduates come back for the game and a reception. There are sure to be some of Bobby's older friends at the match, so I want to do him proud. I shall let you know how it goes. Of course, by the time I write and tell you the news and you receive it, we shall be into basketball season.

I miss your being at my games, Dad.

Yours, Charles

Chapter Six

Charles snorted with laughter. "Ron has to do what?"

Sighing, Wesley repeated: "Teacher's making him stay after school to clean the chalkboard for a month because of his picking on me."

Charles was standing in front of their bedroom's small mirror, combing back his wavy, sandy-colored hair to admire a wide streak of white he'd peroxided into it on Bobby's urging. All the football players had done it for homecoming. He burst out laughing again. "That's rich, that is!"

"It's not funny!" Wesley wailed. "Ron's going to be really gunning for me now. Cleaning the chalkboard won't stop him. You know how it is here. American students don't listen to teachers like we do. They don't even stand when teachers enter the room."

Charles stopped midbrush and studied his younger brother's

reflection in the mirror. "Wes, you have got to toughen up." Charles turned to face his younger brother. "For starters, what were you doing carrying about Mum and Dad's telegram?"

Wesley shrugged and started scratching his arm.

"Stop that!" Charles snapped.

Wesley flopped onto the bed and held the pillow over his face.

Charles sighed and sat down at the foot of the bed. He never seemed to get these heart-to-hearts with his little brother right. What would Dad say to Wes? he wondered. He remembered being told that sticks and stones might break his bones but words would never hurt, that he should rise above insults. Charles had even had to recite that Rudyard Kipling poem about self-control titled "If," the one all good boys of the Empire were supposed to live up to, that claimed if a boy was hated but didn't "give way to hating" then he'd "be a Man."

All well and good, but Wesley needed more than idealistic poetry and nursery sayings. "Listen, Wes, you need to stop being so afraid of Ron. If he clouts you, I'll beat the snot out of him. Trust me."

Wesley peeped out from behind the pillow. "Really?"

"Of course." Charles held up his arm and flexed his new football-honed muscles. He was naturally broad in his shoulders, trim, and long-waisted, a build that high school sports had only enhanced. "Like Popeye, eh?"

Wesley giggled.

"But you must learn to stand up for yourself, Wes. I won't

always be around to bail you out, you know. By the time I turn sixteen, I'm going home to fight, no matter what Mum and Dad say. I figure I can stow away on a tanker out of Norfolk. I'll steal a boat if I have to."

Wesley sat up.

"Now, look, the way to shut up a kid like Ron is to ignore his taunts. Don't feed the fire. It helps to be really good at something people can admire you for. Like cricket for me. Back home, there was a fifth former who ripped on me constantly until I bowled him twice with that googly Dad taught me. So, what makes you a leader among your mates?"

"Well." Wesley paused. He didn't have mates, not like Charles. "The girls all think I'm 'cute as a bug's ear' now because of teacher."

Charles laughed. "That'll do nicely when you're a little older, Wes. But right now you need to think about something you can do that Ron can't so he'll look foolish if he hassles you."

They both were silent for a moment. "What about the spelling bee?" Wesley suggested cautiously.

"Oh! Of course!" Charles said with a sudden cheerleader enthusiasm. "Think about Odysseus, Wes. He wasn't as strong as Achilles, but he was wily. He outsmarted the Trojans with that wooden horse he built and hid in, remember? You're smart like that, Wes. Prove it—win the bloomin' spelling bee."

From downstairs came Bobby's shout: "Hey, Chuck—time to leave for the game!"

Charles clapped Wesley on his back, as if he were a teammate in a football huddle. "Cheer for me, eh?"

Two-four-six-eight, who do we appreciate? Bishop! Bishop! Yaaaaaaaay, Bishop! Cheerleaders bounced up and down, leading the high school fans in chanting.

Even through his leather helmet, Charles could hear the crowd. Oh, that roar was lovely, it was.

He and Bobby had done it! In the game's last five minutes, when it looked like they were going to lose for sure—they were on the fifty-yard line, fourth down with twenty yards to go—Bobby told Charles he was going for a Hail Mary play. "All or nothing," Bobby said cheerfully as his teammates groaned in anxiety in the huddle.

"Right-o, chaps, get a wiggle on!" Charles had echoed Bobby's matter-of-fact gutsiness in the thickest of Briticisms to make the other boys laugh, even though he himself was terrified of flubbing the play.

"Rauuught-oooh," they'd drawled back, trying to smile.

They lined up.

"Twelve . . . forty-one . . . hut!" Bobby called.

The ball snapped into play.

Thunk! Uggh! The linesmen smacked into their opponents to let Charles slip past their wrestling battle.

Charles darted to the left, then to the right, looking over his shoulder to spot Bobby's throw. *There it was!* He hurtled into the air to catch Bobby's bullet pass, somehow landed on his feet, zigzagged around huge farm boys hurling themselves at his knees, and sprinted half the field to cross the goal line.

Touchdown! Charles had scored a touchdown!

All their kicker had to do was get the extra point to lift Bobby's team to a solid three-point lead. He walked onto the field nervously. Along with everyone else in the stadium Charles held his breath as the kicker lined himself up, said a little prayer, and booted the football. It sailed up and up and up and then through the goal posts.

Hurrah! The marching band burst into song. The crowd roared and danced. They shook pom-poms and blew through long herald horns. The bleachers swayed with their stamping.

As Bobby and Charles trotted back to the bench and the defense squad went onto the field, Charles spotted the Ratcliff clan and Wesley in the middle of the stands. He elbowed Bobby to look. The Ratcliffs were going berserk. Sticking his pinkie fingers in his mouth, Mr. Ratcliff whistled in ear-piercing blasts. Mrs. Ratcliff and Patsy hugged, then clapped, then hugged again.

"Hey, look at that, Chuck!" Bobby pointed. The twins had wrapped themselves around Wesley and in a three-way bear hug they jumped up and down, waving at him and Bobby. Then even Ron put his arms around their frolicking circle. "Well, I'll be danged," said Bobby.

Now the opposing team possessed the ball. A touchdown would give them the win. Bobby and Charles and all the other players put their arms over one another's shoulders as the clock ticked down. First down after first down, the other team inched itself toward the goal line.

De-*fense*! Clap, clap. De-*fense*! Clap-clap. The fans chanted.

Fifteen seconds remained on the clock. The opposing team was too far away to kick a field goal to tie the game and throw it into overtime. Their quarterback would have to throw a go-for-broke pass, just as Bobby had. If the other team made the play, it would pull ahead, with no time left for Bobby and Charles's team to retaliate.

The opposing quarterback threw a beautiful, sailing pass. Charles heard Bobby whisper, "Please, Lord, no." Several other players swore.

The ball seemed to hang in the air forever. The wide receiver jumped up and . . . dropped the ball! *Incomplete! The pass was incomplete!* Just as the whistle blew.

The home stands erupted in celebration. They'd won!

Tumbling all over themselves in jubilation, their teammates lifted Charles and Bobby onto their shoulders and danced around the field in a hooting, happy mass. Finally, as their celebration started to wind down, Bobby broke free and grabbed Charles. They ran to the sideline where the Ratcliffs waited, still cheering and waving.

The two friends yanked off their helmets and pumped them up and down in victory as they ran. As he got closer, Charles could see that Wesley's grin stretched ear to ear. Even Ron saluted him.

The family engulfed them in hugs and congratulations. Passed from Ratcliff to Ratcliff, Charles found himself face to face with Patsy. Before he knew what was happening, she threw her arms around his neck and kissed him on his cheek, hugging him tight. "Oh, that was wonderful, Charles! I'm awful proud of you!"

She pulled back and launched herself at Bobby. "Darling, you are something else!"

Laughing, Bobby said, "We better get back to the boys. I just knew Mama would want a hug from her football stud son. Right, Mama?"

"Lord a' mercy. You won't be able to get your head through the door when we get home, I wager!" Mrs. Ratcliff teased.

"Let's go, Chuck." Bobby yanked on his sleeve.

But Charles was rooted, dazed with the scent of Patsy's perfume, the caress of her soft auburn hair against his cheek. He was smiling like an idiot, struck down by a sudden, overwhelming crush.

"Chuck?"

"Eh? Oh. Sorry." He turned with Bobby and jogged toward the locker room.

"Did you get a hit in the head I don't know about, Chuck?" Bobby joked.

Sort of, thought Charles.

It was the best day of his life. The only thing that would top it, Charles thought, was if Hitler dropped dead.

The next week, it was Wesley's chance at glory.

Charles sat midway back in the auditorium and watched his little brother squirm on stage in front of a hundred people. No cheerleaders for this contest, just silent pressure. Lord, thought Charles, this kind of contest didn't seem remotely fun.

He promised himself that he'd be sure to praise Wesley for doing it—he didn't think he'd have the guts for it himself.

Sitting next to Charles was Patsy. Since the game, he'd been rather awkward around her. She was going steady with another bloke. *One off fighting the war, no less,* he reprimanded himself for his crush. Only a rascal would try to snake a girl from a guy off fighting the Jerries. Besides, he had a snowball's chance in hell with the likes of such a beautiful girl. But he still stole a quick glance her way. That only made Charles more unhappy—she was such a dish!

Patsy was smiling encouragement at Wesley. She'd tied his necktie tight and neat for him before the spelling bee, and Charles could tell Wesley was about to suffocate in it. He listened as his brother's competitors successfully made it through their first round words: "cataclysm," "finicky," "necessary," "lectern," "hippopotamus," "bazaar." The words were much harder than Wesley's school spelling bee list had been. Charles noticed Wesley scratch his last remaining swatch of poison ivy. *Steady, lad.* He tried to throw his thoughts up to the stage.

"Wesley Bishop," the moderator called.

Wesley stood.

Charles held up his fist in a gladiator-style salute so his little brother could see him. A small smile crossed Wesley's face. "Come on, Wes," Charles muttered, "for England, to show up Ron."

"Neighbor," said the moderator.

Charles exhaled in relief. *Piece of cake!*

Without hesitation, Wesley rattled off, "N-e-i-g-h-b-o-u-r."

The auditorium crowd gasped.

The three judges conferred, with one lady gesturing toward Wesley and making the kind of sweet face mothers did to coax babies to eat some Pablum. But a bespectacled man shook his head vehemently, forcing the man next to him to agree.

"No, I'm sorry," the moderator said finally. "That is incorrect."

Wesley was excused from the stage.

Americans didn't put a *u* following the *o* in their spelling of "armor," "honor," "rumor," or . . . "neighbor."

Ron smirked.

"God's teeth," muttered Charles.

24 October 1943

Dearest Mummy,

Do not tell Daddy but I botched the spelling bee. On the simplest thing—an American spelling versus our proper British one. I think it humiliated Charles. Now we are coming to another event where I may embarrass him. He and Bobby are hosting a Halloween haunted house. Everyone will come because they are such football heroes now. Plus Yanks do seem to love scaring themselves silly with witches and goblins. I think it is because they have not experienced a REAL fright, not like we Brits have. Last time I went to a haunted house, it reminded me of an Anderson shelter, it was so dark and damp. I vomited on a plate of caramel apples! This year the Ratcliffs want to camp out at a nearby Civil War battlefield, to tell ghost stories!

In school, we are on the War of 1812. It is no better than the Revolution! Did you know we kidnapped American sailors and BURNED the WHITE HOUSE? Honestly, Mummy, it is amazing the Yanks stand by us at all. Ron is now calling me 'limey' since our Royal Navy sucked on limes from the Caribbean colonies to prevent scurvy. I am so WRETCHED, Mummy.

I hope the maple leaf I put in this letter arrives in one piece—it is such a lovely orangey-red. I do not remember anything quite like it back home.

Your devoted son,
Wesley Bishop

Dear Dad,

The latest swivet on this side of the pond is that there will not be candy for Halloween because of sugar rationing! I wonder how long it has been since my mates back home have even seen chocolate. When I return I am bringing them a suitcase of Tootsie Rolls. Is there anything you would like? Tobacco? Richmond must be the capital of cigarette making, but even here ciggies are hard to come by because tobacco is now designated an 'essential crop' for the troops. Mr Ratcliff plans to plant some, even though it ruins soil. I think he is embarrassed about not being able to re-up with the army on account of his limp. So he does whatever he can for the war effort.

Back to Halloween. Mr Ratcliff says if he catches us vandalising anything he will 'tan us good.' Evidently in his day, youth ran wild with 'tricks,' like loosening hinges on gates. When some poor bloke opened it the next day to let out the cows the gate crashed down on his foot. Doling out 'treats' was the American way of stopping such mischief during the Depression when life was already bad enough. To keep everyone out of trouble, Bobby and I are planning a haunted house in the barn. The country is using Halloween celebrations to organise scrap drives. So we will charge everyone some tin cans or old paper to enter. Mr Ratcliff seemed pleased with that idea.

I wish you would tell me what happened at Verdun during the Great War. Mr Ratcliff will not discuss it except to say you were very brave and he is 'mighty beholden' to you. I hope someday we can have a proper talk about it over a cup of Mum's tea. Or a pint! At this rate, I shall be drinking and shaving before I see you again. May I come home now, Dad? The war must be turning our way, at least some, since there are German POWs here now. When I first saw a truckload I started to hurl a rotten apple at them. I wish it had been a grenade.

Love, Charles

Chapter Seven

"I'll need you boys to check the pumpkin patch and load the ripe ones onto the truck tomorrow afternoon so I can drive them into Shockoe. Customers have been coming into Mr. Epstein's store asking for pumpkins to make jack-o'-lanterns." Mr. Ratcliff tipped his wooden chair onto its back legs as he talked to Bobby. "Plan on a big work weekend, son. We've got to cut the corn and shred the stalks for fodder, then plant winter wheat. Somehow got to find time to hay, too."

He patted his stomach and added, "Wonderful chicken dumplings, Mary Lee."

"Thank you kindly, sir," Mrs. Ratcliff said, teasing him as she spooned squash onto the twins' plates. "Eat up now, honeys. No arguing. There are plenty of children who'd be grateful for that extra helping of squash. It'll make you big and strong."

Wesley moved his elbow so Mrs. Ratcliff could ladle a spoonful onto his plate too. Squash was an American vegetable

Wesley tried hard to like, especially after learning its importance to the Indians' diet, but he still gagged over its limp seeds. He took a few bites. Then he carefully spread the remnants around his plate to look like he'd eaten most of it.

He noticed Patsy watching him with an amused smile. She held a plate of still-warm bread toward him. "Roll?" she asked. Wesley gratefully took one, wondering if she'd guessed what he was doing with the squash.

"Ah, that'll be tough, Dad," Bobby said, as he reached across and grabbed the last roll, beating Ron to it. "Chuck and I have football practice for championships. And Saturday we need to set up the barn and make guts and stuff for our haunted house. Can't Ed help you?"

Mr. Ratcliff lowered his chair legs back to the floor. He leaned forward. "Robert, I am proud of your football record. Very proud, son. But I need you. Ed will already be helping. You know this time of year I usually hire extra field hands in addition to Ed. But I can't find any—they've all joined up, or work in the factories, or have gone down to Newport News shipyards. Ed's sons, too."

"They're hiring Negroes at the docks?" Ron asked.

Mr. Ratcliff seemed to consider his middle son carefully before answering. "I'd hate to think you harbor some of the bass-ackwards attitudes others around here have, Ronald. We need every able body to help in this war, either in the armed services or in the jobs that keep them going. I know Richmond gentry are squawking over their help going AWOL. But I applaud the Negroes taking the opportunity to get better jobs. About the only good thing in this war is that it's finally opening doors for them that were glued shut before. I hear they can make fifty-eight cents an hour at the Yorktown Naval Yard. That's double what they're used to being paid. We should be glad for them."

"Fifty-eight cents an hour?" exclaimed Mrs. Ratcliff. "Lord love a duck. If I didn't have so much canning and preserving to do right now, I'd get myself a job."

Her sons stopped eating, forks halfway to their mouths, to stare at her.

"Boys, I had a perfectly good secretary job before your father and I married," she countered, a bit miffed. "Why do you look so surprised?"

"You're just such a good mama," said Bobby, "it's hard for us to see you any other way. I always think of you playing hide-and-seek with us behind the sheets when you hung them to dry on the clothesline and never yelling at us if we got dirt on them during the game."

"Well, aren't you the sweetest thing, honey. But that's beside the point. I am a trained stenographer, you know. Your daddy and I met at the bank, after all."

"Tell the story again, Daddy," Patsy prompted him.

The twins clapped their hands. "Tell us, Daddy."

Mr. Ratcliff leaned back in his chair again. "Well, well. There I was behind my desk approving a loan for some fat-cat lawyer—one of the first loans my daddy let me process. He was president of the bank, if you remember."

"We do, Daddy," sung the twins.

"So it was a right big moment in my youthful career, a serious moment, a moment I became a real banker in my own right. A moment to be dignified and mature."

Bobby stifled a laugh.

"Never mind him, Daddy." Patsy slapped Bobby's arm. "Do tell."

"Well, as I was saying." He cleared his throat and smiled at Mrs. Ratcliff. "There I was at a moment of import. The ink was drying on the documents, and I was about to stand up, shake the old lawyer's hand, and hand him a Cuban. I reached into the drawer for the cigar, when the front door to the bank atrium opened, light flooded in, and there stood this gorgeous, I mean breathtaking, gal. She wore a lilac-colored suit and had the prettiest little hat perched on her auburn curls, and leeeeggs that went all the way down to here." He patted the floor.

"Oh, for goodness' sake, Andy, where else would my legs go?" But Mrs. Ratcliff blushed and laughed all the same.

"Do you remember what happened next?" he asked his children, making a silly face.

"You fell right out of your chair," the twins shouted, giggling.

"Yes sirree, Bob, I sure did. Right on my keister. I was one cooked goose right then and there. My heart was hers." He reached for her hand and kissed it. "Always has been."

"Awwwww." Patsy, the twins, and Wesley sighed.

Mr. Ratcliff wagged a finger at his sons. "You be sure to find a lady like this one to love. She hasn't complained once about my family losing the bank during the Depression or about my having to turn to farming or about my bum leg keeping me from taking her dancing."

"And why would I, Andy, when I have you and five such beautiful children, aaaannnnd"—she drew out the word—"lovely British guests to boot." She stood to clear dishes.

Mr. Ratcliff watched her a moment and then turned with earnestness to Patsy. "And you make sure, sweetheart, that your husband loves and respects you as much as I do your mama."

Mrs. Ratcliff came back with some fried apples for dessert. "You know I could get a job if they're offering that much in wages, Andy. Truly."

"Mama," Patsy interrupted. "You're already volunteering with the Red Cross rolling surgical bandages. I should be the one to get a job. I can't be that much help in the fields. I've heard Bellwood is hiring women. I can ride my bike there after school."

"Bellwood? That's no place for a girl, Pats," said Bobby. "There are a thousand Nazi POWs there now."

Charles saw Patsy bristle. Maybe it was because she'd grown up running with a pack of brothers, but Patsy was always infuriated by any implication girls weren't as brave as boys. Most of the girls around the high school always acted so helpless and kind of silly. Not Patsy. She had a tomboy grin and didn't bother to pluck her eyebrows or perm her hair like the other girls either. Charles really liked that about her.

"Oh really?" Patsy pointed her fork at Bobby. "I'll have you know that Meredith was just hired as a chauffeur. And she told me that they were hiring women as storekeepers and secretaries, even as guards. What about all those magazines celebrating Rosie the Riveter?"

"Back home, my mum is a volunteer ambulance driver," Charles spoke up.

Patsy smiled gratefully at Charles. "There, you see, Daddy?" she said.

Mr. Ratcliff frowned. "Pshaw, this war is going to take us to hell in a handbasket. Women working at a depot knee-deep in soldiers and POWs. What next?"

The Ratcliff brothers nodded in agreement.

Patsy's cheeks turned red under her freckles, but she folded her hands together like in prayer, and took a deep breath before speaking. "Daddy," she said, "I am perfectly capable of taking care of myself. Don't you remember the time the truck had a flat when I was running the twins to Aunt Mamie's, and I changed it myself? And the time that I—"

"Hold on, girl." Mr. Ratcliff held up his hand to quiet her. As generous as he was, Charles knew Mr. Ratcliff did not like his authority to be questioned. He kept his hand up for a moment. It was calloused from hoeing and fixing farm machinery. But his voice softened to courtliness as he continued, making it easy for Charles to imagine Mr. Ratcliff behind a desk in a vaulted, elegant bank building once upon a time.

"You're busy getting your education, honey. You're the smartest among us. I'd give just about anything to have the money to pay your college tuition, but the reality is you will need a scholarship." He patted his daughter's hand. "You focus on that. I just know you'll be an outstanding teacher or librarian or nurse one day." He turned to his eldest son. "I just need Robert, here, to be responsible. I need help with our fields."

Bobby sighed. "Okay, Dad. I understand. But everyone's got to chip in, then, with setting up the haunted house Halloween morning."

"Sure thing, Bobby," chirped the twins.

"Now, hold on a minute." Mrs. Ratcliff had a thought. "Isn't the thirty-first on Sunday this year?" Mrs. Ratcliff was a devout Methodist. One of the first things Bobby had told Charles was that their attic room would be the main hang on Sunday afternoons so they could play gin rummy without getting caught playing cards on church day.

"Mary Lee, sweetheart, there's a war on," said her husband. "Sabbath rules will have to bend for a while. If I am only able to get help on the weekends, that's when I'm mowing the hay—Sunday or not. As it is, even with our sons helping, I'm hard pressed to get things harvested before they rot. We'll have our first hard frost any day now. I can't afford our last timothy hay and clover being ruined because I can't get it cut and baled in time. I've already lost more than two hundred dollars profit that I should have made on my corn, thanks to that drought. How it didn't rain for fifty-seven days straight is beyond me."

He paused. "In fact," he began cautiously, "I've been mulling something over. Some farmers around the county have hired work details of POWs from Camp Pickett to help them hay. I might need to do so as well."

Instantly, he was pounded with a chorus of protests: "What?" "Nazis?" "In our fields?" "Near our house?" "Are you nuts, Dad?"

Mr. Ratcliff might as well have dropped an incendiary bomb on the table as far as Charles was concerned. Without thinking, he stood abruptly, knocking his chair over.

Startled, everyone silenced. They waited for him to speak. But he couldn't. How could Charles explain that if a Nazi was within one hundred yards of him, he might grab the nearest pitchfork and gut the guy? How could anyone explain feeling that kind of bitter, murderous rage? He just shook his head. Then he ran from the room, slamming the back door behind him.

"Poor lamb," said Mrs. Ratcliff. "Andy, you should have thought how that might upset Charles."

"Yeah, Dad," Bobby piped up. "Chuck told me that five of his neighbors died in just one night during the Blitz. And that only about half the houses on his block were still in one piece before he left to come here. He was pretty torn up about it. I don't know how he and Wes withstood it all."

"I can't imagine any Londoner being able to stand the sight of a German right now," said Patsy.

Even Ron appeared sympathetic.

"Now, wait just a minute," Mr. Ratcliff defended himself. "It's not like I have any love for the German empire. Kaiser Wilhelm wasn't exactly good to me." He shifted in his chair and tucked his bad leg under the table. "I just haven't many choices these days."

Wesley looked from face to face, wondering if they remembered that he was sitting right there among them. He rose to follow Charles. He had no idea what to say to his big brother. Always trying to keep that stiff upper lip, Charles got angry whenever he realized Wesley knew that he was upset. But the moment seemed to call for some British brother solidarity.

"Andy." Mrs. Ratcliff looked pointedly at her husband as she said his name. She reached out without taking her eyes off her husband and gently caught Wesley's arm, stopping him.

Mr. Ratcliff heaved a sigh. "All right, all right. How much is in that mason jar, Mary Lee?"

She smiled fondly at her husband. "I just counted that up yesterday as a matter of fact. Eighteen whole dollars and thirteen cents."

The Ratcliff boys whistled. "You've been holding out on us, Mama," teased Bobby.

"For a rainy day, sugar," she answered.

Humph. Mr. Ratcliff pretended to peer out the window to assess the clouds. Then he turned to Wesley. "How about you find Chuck and then you two go ask Ed if his sons can catch the Greyhound from the shipyards this weekend. I'll cover the bus tickets and pay wages and a half if they can work both days, all day, including Sunday, until every scrap of hay is baled, every cornstalk is shredded, and the wheat is planted and the fields put to bed for the winter."

"Yes, sir!" Wesley answered.

Mr. Ratcliff turned to Bobby. "But even with Ed and his sons, I'll need your help to get everything done in time." He made eye contact with each boy, one by one. "All of yours—Robert, Ronald, John, James—this weekend."

They all nodded solemnly, even the twins.

"Might send me to the poorhouse," Mr. Ratcliff muttered, "but it'll keep me from hiring POWs." He smiled at his wife. "All right?"

Mrs. Ratcliff let go of Wesley's hand to hug her husband.

Out in the yard, Wesley went around and around trying to locate Charles. He wasn't in the grape arbor, or the woodshed, or the smokehouse, or the orchard, or down by the chicken houses. Wesley searched the barn, climbing into the hayloft, where once he'd caught Charles and Bobby choking on hand-rolled chicory cigarettes. Charles was simply nowhere to be found.

Maybe he's gone as far as the river, thought Wesley, starting for the path that wound through the woods to the pebbly banks of the James. He knew the river was where Charles often went to hurl rocks when he was mad, gaining some satisfaction from the enormous splashes they made in the choppy waters. Sometimes Charles even waded up to his knees and gazed east down its murky, urgent waves, saying that beyond their view the river gaped open to be five miles across and gushed into the Chesapeake Bay and the Atlantic beyond. "That way's home," he'd tell Wesley, as the waves lapped hard against his legs so that Charles had to brace himself against the tide's push.

Once, Charles even speculated that he could float a raft down to Hampton Roads if he caught the tides right. "Just like that Huck Finn did the Mississippi," Charles had said, more to himself than to Wesley. "Bet I could do it in a night and climb onto a ship without anyone seeing me in the dark." Charles had stood for a long time, as if in a trance.

Remembering that episode, Wesley stopped himself. Charles wasn't going to listen to him if he were in that kind of mood. And he was sure to be. Wouldn't it be better for Wesley to actually have good news to tell Charles for once, like that he'd prevented Mr. Ratcliff from bringing in POWs by talking to Ed?

Suddenly, Wesley felt rather important. He turned and jogged toward the old sharecroppers' cottage where Ed and his wife, Alma, lived.

Twilight was dropping as Wesley came to Ed's four-room cottage. Half log cabin, half whitewashed board, its happiest feature was a long ramshackle porch across its front that doubled its size. A long neat line of white river rocks marked the path to the front door, which Alma ringed with marigolds in the summer. She worked hard, long hours as a maid at one of the old river mansions down the road, but when Alma was home, the scent of something good cooking always greeted Wesley as he passed on the way to school. Sometimes she even handed the Ratcliff boys biscuits to eat on their way.

"It's okay," Bobby reassured them when Wesley and Charles worried over taking food from someone who clearly had so little. "She misses her own children. It makes her feel better." Alma's four sons were all grown and long gone about their own lives.

Wesley saw a sudden glow inside the cottage as Alma or Ed lit a kerosene lamp for the evening. Good, they're home, he thought, and picked up his pace. As he reached the porch, he heard a cranking sound, then the scratchy *Crrrrrrr-crrrrrr-crrrr* of a record player starting up

A low, mournful voice began to sing: *"Sometimes I feel like a motherless child."* Rising and falling, the voice repeated the lament and then was joined by other deep, sad voices singing, *"A long ways from home . . ."*

Wesley stopped mid-step. The song tore at his heart. He'd never heard music like it before. Sudden hot tears stung his face as Wesley backed away from the sound of someone putting words to his sorrow.

In the gloom, he stumbled and fell back onto the sharp, hard edges of the walkway rocks. "Oooooowwww!" he cried, rolling and clutching his butt, his hip, his elbow, his shoulder. "Oooooowwww!"

In mid roll, Wesley heard another sound—the harsh *cliiiiiick* as the hammer of a gun was cocked and readied.

He sat up.

There on the porch was a boy, holding a shotgun aimed straight at Wesley.

Chapter Eight

"Don't shoot!" Wesley threw up his hands. "Please don't shoot."

The gun didn't lower.

"I—I," he stammered. "I'm terribly sorry if I disturbed you."

Still the boy didn't respond.

"My name is Wesley Bishop." His words rushed out, panicked. "I am staying with the Ratcliffs. Miss Alma knows me. Her biscuits are brilliant!"

At that, the boy peeked out from behind the gun. "You talk funny," he said as he lowered the shotgun, resting its butt against the porch floor.

The two stared at each other. Because the boy was backlit by the lamp, Wesley couldn't see his expression.

Finally, the boy with the gun asked, "So? What do you want?"

Wesley's heartbeat began to slow down enough that he could talk some sense. "Mr. Ratcliff would like to know if Ed's sons might be able to come up from Newport News and help him this weekend. Is he home?"

"Does it look like he's home?" the boy countered. "He's at a church meeting."

"When will he be back?"

"Soon enough." The boy didn't stir.

This was not getting him anywhere. Cautiously, Wesley stood and brushed himself off. His elbow was throbbing and bleeding where a stone had gouged it. He hated to make more work for Mrs. Ratcliff with bloodstains on his clothes. "Might I trouble you for a bandage and some Mercurochrome?" he asked.

"'*Might I trouble you?*'" The boy snorted. "Where you from?"

"Great Britain."

"You came *here* from England?"

"Yes, that's right," Wesley answered hopefully.

"Well, there's a fool born a minute," the boy muttered, taking a step back. "All right, then. Come on in." He dragged the gun behind him and opened the screened door. Wesley followed.

"Don't have Mercurochrome. But you can wash up there." The boy pointed toward the kitchen, where there was a long wooden table with a pitcher and water basin.

Now Wesley could see the boy. He was slight and wiry and wore round horn-rimmed glasses that made his brown eyes seem enormous. Probably just a year or so older, Wesley judged. The boy watched as Wesley rinsed his arm. Then he wandered into the next room to an old wind-up Victrola—the kind of record player with a big trumpet bell coming up from the turntable box.

So that's what Wesley had heard. "What were you listening to?" he asked. "I've never heard music like that before."

"It's a spiritual."

"What's a spiritual?"

"Why, a spiritual is gospel music. A song Negroes sung when we worked fields in our days of bondage. Music helped us get by. This one is 'Motherless Child.' That was the Golden Gate Quartet singing it. They're the famous jubilee group from Norfolk, you know."

Wesley admitted he didn't.

"What? The Golden Gate sang at the last inauguration of President Franklin Delano Roosevelt himself! They're the first Negro music group to sing in Constitution Hall and the White House!"

The boy turned to a small stack of thick records and rifled through them indignantly. "Didn't you see the movie *Star Spangled Rhythm*? They performed in that with Mary Martin and Dick Powell." Finally, the boy found what he was looking for. Ever so carefully, he took the first record off the turntable, slipped it into a sleeve, and replaced it with the one he'd located. "This is their latest. For sure you know this one." He cranked the box's handle and gently put the needle onto the rotating black disk.

Crrrrrrr-crrrrrrr-crrrrr...

Four men began to sing in tight, deep harmony about Stalin, the "Russian Bear," and the Soviets standing up to Hitler's invasion and blockade. It sounded a little like the *a capella* barbershop quartets Wesley had heard at the county fair. But the rhythms were jauntier and syncopated:

They'd never rest contented
Till they'd driven him from the land....

"Oh, I do know this," Wesley said over the music as the quartet sang that the devil had made Hitler and called Stalin a "noble" Russian. He'd heard it on the radio. Ron had called the singers "a bunch of Reds" for praising the Soviet Union's communist leader Joseph Stalin. Many Americans hated Stalin despite the fact the Soviet Union was one of the Allies and Stalin was labeled one of its "Big Three" leaders, along with FDR and Churchill. After all, once Stalin had aligned with Hitler to divide Poland between them, and his regime was about as repressive as Hitler's Third Reich.

Wesley didn't mention Ron's opinion. Instead he marveled at how the four voices blended, swelled, and fell as one.

Crrrrr-crrrrr-crrrrrr... The music ended.

"Oh that's bully, that is," said Wesley.

The boy's face turned from a look of blissful appreciation of the song to a sudden defensiveness. "No one's trying to bully you, boy."

"Oh no, I mean it's excellent!" Wesley said. He smiled. "I never heard music like this back home in England. We have singers like Vera Lynn. Her best song is 'White Cliffs of Dover.' The cliffs are the last thing our RAF fighters see as they head for bombing runs over Jerryville, and the song is sad and sweet at the same time, about peace coming someday." Wesley stopped abruptly, realizing the boy was frowning. "Do you know the tune?"

The boy shook his head.

"No? Well, anyway, your music . . . well . . . that first song . . . that first song . . ." Wesley hesitated to be honest about the song's effect on him.

The boy completed his thought for him: "Made your heart hurt?"

"Yes," Wesley gasped. "Exactly."

The boy nodded. They were silent a moment.

"Where's your mama?" the boy asked.

Wesley sighed. "Way across the Atlantic Ocean in London."

The boy whistled. "Nerts! For real?"

Wesley nodded. "Where's yours?"

"Down to Newport News Shipbuilding and Dry Dock Company." The boy used the long company name with noticeable pride. "She and my daddy both are building warships. Virginia is popping them out fast now. Daddy got hired as a welder. Mama paints the hulls." He eyed Wesley. "What do your folks do?"

"Daddy is a teacher and coach, and a volunteer fireman. He pulls people out of buildings that the Nazis have bombed. Mummy drives an ambulance."

The boy pursed his lips and nodded, showing Wesley that, at least as far as his parents' war-worthiness, he checked out. "Why aren't you with your parents?" Wesley asked.

"I was," the boy explained. "But the company is hiring so fast there's a terrible housing shortage. Landlords get away with charging eight dollars a week for a one-bedroom apartment. Don't that beat all? My parents needed to take in another couple to help pay that. Besides, Mama was so tired when she came home—after standing for eight hours with only twenty minutes for a lunch break—she had nothing left for me, she said. So she sent me here to Grandpop and Gran. I wanted to go back to our own house, but . . ." He lowered his voice and said in a conspiratorial whisper, "The government took it."

"What?" Wesley asked. "Why?"

"They're building something secret."

"Where?"

"A ways yonder," he gestured over this shoulder. "About ten mile toward Richmond Air Base and Elko."

"What are they building?"

The boy shrugged. "Don't know for sure. But I'm pretty sure I saw the shape of a plane of some kind, covered up with netting."

"You don't say?" Wesley wondered at that mystery for a moment. "Why would they do that?"

The boy shrugged again. "Beats me." So much was hushed up because of the war.

"But they just took your land?"

"That's right. Came one day and told us and all our neighbors that we had to leave in thirty days. They tried to set us up in a trailer camp instead. 'Shucks,' my daddy said. He'd rather work at the docks anyway, helping with the war. Just like my uncles. Daddy has three brothers. Every last one a true-blue patriot." He held up a finger with each description: "The youngest is training in Norfolk. He'll ship out soon with the navy as a messman on a destroyer or an aircraft carrier. Uncle Chester is a wiper on merchant ships. He's back and forth, on the Atlantic, dodging U-boats, taking troops the supplies they need to keep fighting. Like I said, my daddy builds fighting ships. It's a cause with my daddy since his big brother died. Uncle Walter was out just past Norfolk, without any navy boys to protect them and..."

The screen door opened, interrupting the boy. Alma and Ed entered, dressed in their Sunday best.

"Wesley!" Alma said in surprise. "Everything all right with the family?"

"Oh, yes." Wesley stood up. "Mr. Ratcliff sent me to ask if you and your sons might be able to help him hay." He explained Mr. Ratcliff's offer of bus fare and time-and-a-half wages. "Otherwise he'll need to hire POWs from Camp Pickett... and it's just... well, it'll be hard for Charles to be around Nazis." Wesley stopped short of admitting that he didn't exactly want to be around men who might have dropped bombs on his homeland either.

Ed took off his fedora and suit coat and sat down heavily in a rocking chair. He was a strong man, but elderly and stiff, with deep long lines in his face from working in the sun. He undid his bow tie as he spoke. "I'll get them word. I'm not keen on Nazis being around here myself, not after losing our boy Walter with the *Atwater*."

Wesley took in a sharp breath. Everyone knew the story of

the *Atwater*. Its sinking was probably the most notorious torpedoing of any American cargo ship. Carrying tons of coal, the *Atwater* had steamed out of Norfolk all alone, its crew unaware of being shadowed by a Nazi submarine. Right after nightfall, just off Chincoteague, the U-boat opened fire, shelling the ship's bridge and engines. The *Atwate*r burst into flames and sunk in fifteen minutes. But the Nazis kept firing on the crew.

"Nazis don't have any hearts, I'd say," muttered the boy. "How could they shoot at *Atwater* sailors when all those poor fools were trying to do was put on life preservers and jump into the water. They'd already sunk the boat and all its coal."

"The Nazis even gunned down one of the lifeboats," added Ed, sadness lacing his voice. "By the time the coast guard got there, most everyone had drowned or bled to death." He shook his head. "Including our Walt."

Wesley remembered that newspapers had called the Nazis' firing on unarmed men and the lifeboats nothing short of cold-blooded murder. Secretly, he and Charles had felt a twinge of bizarre satisfaction when reading that commentary. Now Americans knew how cruel, how unrelenting fanatical Nazis could be. Maybe now they would understand better what Londoners had withstood night after bloody night during the Blitz, when Hitler had targeted civilians for no strategic purpose other than terror. They were hardly charity cases the way Ron—and some others—painted them.

But now Wesley felt really bad. Before, the sinking of the *Atwater* had been just an event that vindicated him and Charles—like a plot twist that helped characters recognize an important truth. Now it was real. Now he knew people who had a hole ripped in their hearts and wept at night because of it. Just like at home.

For a long, uncomfortable moment, Ed, Alma, the boy, and Wesley remained silent. Finally, Wesley found his voice and, for once, the right thing to say. "It's jolly brave of your other son to keep sailing on the cargo ships."

Ed blew his nose.

Alma smiled. "Yes. My boys are special. Every last one of them."

"I keep telling him he doesn't need to volunteer to sail them sitting ducks," said Ed.

"Read him Uncle Chester's letter, Gran, from his last sail," the boy suggested.

"Oh no, Wesley doesn't have time for that."

"I'd like to hear it," Wesley answered. "Truly."

"All right." Alma walked to an old bureau and pulled out a letter from a drawer. Holding it in the lamp's glow, she carefully read:

"'Dear Mama and Daddy, I can't sleep because nights are when the Nazi tin fish come out. So I figured I'd write. Today we had a lifeboat drill. Know what? If we got to jump ship we need to remember to hold down our lifebelt as we fall. If we don't the belt's like to jerk up and break our necks when we hit the water. So here we are, risking getting blown to bits and the thing that is supposed to save us can kill us! I swear any lame-brained fool shipping out these days has bubbles in his think tank.

"'Sometimes we all wonder why we do it. No one treats us

merchant sailors to USO shows! But here's the thing, Mama. I reckon you can use my war bonus of $2.33 a day. Save it up and send Freddy to Howard College. Tell him his Uncle Chess says so—I've seen how many books that boy reads. Besides, we've got to keep the tankers sailing to get our boys supplies while they're fighting. We don't want swastikas flying over the U.S. instead of Old Glory!

"'Plus, we colored boys in the crew have been talking. Maybe at the end of this war, the Negro can get credit for what we do now. Maybe we can finally prove to the country that courage has no color.'"

Alma folded the letter and kissed it. Hearing it embarrassed and inspired Wesley all at the same time. He knew it was the time for him to leave.

The boy walked him to the door.

"Are you Freddy?" Wesley asked.

"Yes."

"You like books?"

Freddy nodded.

"Ever read *Treasure Island*? That's my favorite."

"Never heard of it."

"What? Well, I shall lend you my copy." Wesley extended his hand to shake in a gesture of friendliness Americans seemed so at ease with. "Pleased to meet you."

Freddy looked at Wesley's hand with surprise, then took it. *"Shall?"* He made a face like he'd just bitten into a sour apple. Then he grinned, showing he was teasing, and imitated Wesley's clipped British accent. "Pleased to meet you."

They laughed.

Wesley stepped off the porch and let his eyes adjust to the moonlight. It was a fairly new moon rising and didn't give off much light. Even so, Wesley fairly skipped on his way home. Not only did he have good news for Charles, Wesley might actually have made a friend.

Chapter Nine

"Walk on!" Bobby shouted. Standing behind a plow, he faced the rear end of two mules. He snapped one of the long reins he held so the strap rippled forward along its length to whack one of the animals' rumps.

The mule snorted and bobbed his head. But he didn't budge.

Bobby flipped the other rein so it snapped the butt of the other mule. She laid her ears back and swished her tail. But she didn't move either. "Aw, g'on, Belle!" He clucked.

Hee-haw, hee-haw. Belle seemed to laugh.

Bobby kicked the dirt. "I can't believe there's not enough gas for the tractor! We're getting nowhere with these ornery jackasses. This is ridiculous." He let go of the plow's handles and cupped his hands to his mouth. "Dad!" he shouted. "Dad-dyyyyy!"

"That's real smart, Bobby," said Ron. "As if Dad could hear you over the shredder."

Up by the barn's silo, Mr. Ratcliff and Ed were shoving acres of cut cornstalks into a buzz-saw shredder. Across the fields, Ed's sons and two of their friends were raking and pitchforking mown hay into a tractor baler. Those machines were using the only rationed gas Mr. Ratcliff had left for the month, even though he had an "essential farmer" quota.

So it was up to the boys to turn over the soil of the shorn cornfields to plant winter wheat the old fashioned way—with a heavy plow pulled by a pair of mules. For a Londoner, this kind of work was all new and shockingly hard. Bobby was trying to guide the iron blade to cut the earth in a relatively straight furrow between the old corn rows. The corn stubble would actually shield the tender wheat shoots from frosty winds and prevent winterkill—a brilliant bit of practical thinking, but one that required precision. The mules' resistance was turning the already backbreaking task into a terrible battle.

"Okay, Mr. Big Shot, go take Belle by the bridle," Bobby directed Ron. "If we can get her to move, Jake will follow." Bobby pulled off his work gloves and, holding them up like a riding crop, positioned himself by the mule's rear end. "Chuck, you take hold of the plow for a few minutes."

Charles had been walking behind Bobby with a sack of seed, tossing handfuls into the freshly churned ground. Following him, Wesley and Ron had been raking soil on top of the seed, while the twins tiptoed behind, pressing down the dirt so it wouldn't blow away and expose the seed to hungry birds. Even though Bobby called him a city slicker, Charles knew to safeguard the precious seed from spilling. Before taking hold of the plow's splintery handles, he hung the burlap sack on Wesley's shoulder. "Be careful with that," he warned. Then he stepped into Bobby's post behind the mules.

With Ron yanking on her bridle and Bobby smacking her butt, Belle moved. Jake did follow. But within moments Charles knew exactly why the mules had stopped dead before. In ten strides, they stepped on an underground yellow-jacket nest, its entrance hole covered with weeds. A few seconds later those mules were covered with dozens of mad, stinging wasps.

Hee-haw, hee-haw! The animals lurched forward, bucking in panic, straining against the plow's lines to break free from the pain.

Ron jumped aside and ran away, hollering and swatting yellow jackets off himself.

Bobby stayed with the kicking, lunging mules, even though Charles could see he was being swarmed. "Whoaaaaa now, Belle. Easy, Jake." Bobby's voice was somehow calm.

Charles followed his friend's lead and stuck to his post. He pulled back on the long reins with all his might. But he was no match for the mules' panicked strength. They yanked Charles forward, bashing his chest against the top crossbeam of the plow.

"God's teeth!" Charles cursed, barely able to breathe from the blow. But he righted himself and planted his feet. He wrapped the reins once, twice around his hands to have a better grip—just like he'd done in games of tug-of-war at his London boys' school. He wasn't about to be bested by two mules.

But instinct ruled the mules now. Belle knocked Bobby to

the ground as she fought against the plow's harness. Jake reared and bucked, reared and bucked.

SNAP! The chain connecting the mules to the plow broke. They bolted. The mules were free.

Charles was not.

Pulled by the leather tied around his hands, Charles vaulted into the air. He hit the dirt face-first. Charles felt himself being dragged, fast, over grasses and cornstalk roots. Spluttering, choking on soil, he tried desperately to worm his wrists free from the leather handcuffs he'd made for himself.

Behind him somewhere, he heard Wesley screaming, "Charles!"

"Let go of the reins, Chuck!" Bobby called. "Let go!"

"Stop, stop, stop!" shrieked the twins.

Spooked by the shouts, the mules only ran faster.

Charles managed to pull himself up enough so his face was at least off the ground. He could see Ed's cottage coming up fast, and behind it, the road. This will be a bloody stupid way to die, Charles thought as he bounced and slid and fought to release himself. He could just hear the lads back home. They'll have a laugh won't they—*Charles Bishop ran away from the Nazis, only to have his neck broken behind a mule's backside!*

"Chuck! Let go the reins!" Bobby's voice was much farther back now.

Charles thought his arms might pull out of their sockets. About two hundred yards to the roadway now.

Suddenly the mules stopped short—like a switch had been flipped off.

Charles heard Bobby thunder up behind him, felt Bobby uncoil the leather straps and yank him away from the reins' hold. "You all right, Chuck? You hurt?"

Charles was scraped up and his clothes were torn, but he seemed to be in one piece.

"Charles!" Wesley ran up, panting. "Thank goodness. You're alive!"

He was followed by the twins.

"Can you walk, Chuck?" Bobby asked as he pulled Charles to his feet and held him up.

Charles took a few wobbly steps, supported by Bobby. "I'm okay," he said feebly. "What stopped them?"

Wesley pointed at a silent, solemn boy the mules were nuzzling, now completely calm. "It's Freddy!"

Wesley was making introductions as Ron stormed up, shouting about being stung.

Bobby ignored him. "I'm mighty grateful to you, Freddy. How'd you stop those jackass mules anyway?"

Freddy shrugged, holding out a piece of cornbread. "Happened to have some leftovers in my pocket. Main thing, though, is not to act like a jackass yourself and be making so much noise around them when they're already scared."

Bobby laughed. "True enough! Well, thank you. I think you might have saved old Chuck's life here."

He still had his arm around Charles, propping him. "Let's get you back to the house, Chuck, and let Mama give you a once-over just to be sure nothing's busted." Slowly Bobby turned

Charles and guided his steps toward the farmhouse. He called back over his shoulder: "Ron, get the mules back to the barn."

"What the hell?" Ron blurted. "Did you hear me say I got stung bad?"

"Yeah, I heard. I've stings on me, too." Bobby kept walking with Charles.

"Not as many as me! I got 'em all over." Ron darted ahead of them and planted himself in front of Bobby. "Look!" His arms were red and blotchy and swelling up fast. "I'm the one you should be helping!"

"Just like you helped me when the mules were rearing and kicking? Just like you helped Chuck when they bolted and he was being dragged? You made the choice to turn tail and look after yourself. So you just keep on doing that." Bobby sidestepped Ron and continued to the house with Charles.

Ron stood watching them for a moment, balling and unballing his fists. Wesley thought he heard Ron muttering, "I'm your brother, not him." But before Wesley could tell for sure, Ron stomped toward the house. He shouted back over his shoulder, "You take care of the mules, limey."

"Shoo-ee." Freddy whistled. "That one's trouble."

"You can say that again," Wesley replied.

"Shoo-ee," Freddy repeated with a grin. "That one's trouble."

He helped Wesley take the mules back to the barn. The boys unharnessed them and hosed their sting-welts with cold well water. "See you later?" Wesley asked as Freddy headed back to Ed's house.

"Not if I see you sooner."

It was an old joke, but Wesley knew it was the kind friends made and were polite enough to laugh over. This was turning out to be a good day! he thought happily. Charles didn't die, and it looked liked Freddy might become a real chum.

Back at the house, Wesley found Charles sitting in a rocker on the porch. His arms were bandaged and Patsy was pressing a wet washcloth against his eye. "It's going to be a proper shiner," Charles told Wesley with a grin.

Bobby and Ron sat on the stoop, and seemed to be ignoring each other. Both were slathered with a paste of baking soda and water to pull the venom out of their stings. Wesley had to admit he didn't feel the least bit sorry for Ron, though he knew he should. He told Bobby that he'd put the mules away and fed them.

"Thanks, Wes, you're a real chum," said Bobby, copying the Bishops' lingo for once.

Wesley could see Ron seethe. He changed the subject before Ron thought up something nasty to say. "Where are the twins?"

"I sent them to the woods to look for Halloween props," answered Bobby, perking up with the thought of his party. "Mulberries to mush into bowls to look like guts, and monkey balls for brains." Bobby burst out laughing at his own accidentally off-color joke.

Monkey balls were wrinkled, green, grapefruit-size fruit of the Osage orange tree that grew wild everywhere in the woods.

When they'd arrived in the States, Wesley and Charles had thought them one of the weirdest-looking things they'd ever seen.

"We're going to blindfold people and get them to stick their hands in stuff as we lead them through blackout curtains," Bobby continued. "You and the twins get to sit in the corners and moan. Like this, *Whoo-a, whoo-a, whoo-a.*" He waved his hands in Ron's face, then elbowed his younger brother. Wesley knew he was trying to make peace. Bobby was like that.

But Ron continued to sulk.

"Honestly, you boys," said Patsy. "Don't you have anything better to do?"

Bobby grinned at her. "Nope."

She rolled her eyes, but laughed all the same. She took the washcloth from Charles's face. "That's going to be black and blue. Thank goodness nothing worse happened."

She went inside. Charles let out a long sigh.

Wesley almost asked his brother if the Ratcliffs had given him a shot of whiskey for pain, he was acting so dopey. But he had another question: "Hey, Bobby, may I invite Freddy to the haunted house?"

Bobby's smile vanished.

"The Negro boy?" Ron nearly shouted.

"Freddy, yes," Wesley answered.

"Do you know what my friends would say if..."

Bobby held up his hand to cut off Ron. "I'm sorry, Wes. Not tonight."

"Why not tonight?"

Bobby looked at the ground for a moment and then back up to Wesley. "If it were just us, or on any other night, I'd say for sure. Honest. But . . ." He paused. "There're definitely some people coming tonight who wouldn't like it, and Halloween's an especially bad night to invite Freddy, Wes. People do stupid things on Halloween. You have to trust me on this."

It was one of the few times Wesley had ever seen Bobby look uncomfortable and unsure of himself. Wesley knew that black children had to attend a different school from the whites, but this was a party at their house. And hadn't Freddy just kept the mules from running into the road and maybe being hit by a truck? He might have even saved Charles's neck.

Ron folded his arms and smirked.

Wesley looked to his big brother. Come on, Charles, say something, he thought.

But Charles didn't.

Chapter Ten

"Sure was nice of Mr. Epstein to give us these marshmallows his wife cooked." Bobby was helping the twins put two homemade marshmallows onto long sticks to hold into the campfire the boys had built near Malvern Hill, the Civil War battlefield. "She must have used up all her sugar ration for these."

He sat Jamie and Johnny down at a safe distance from the flames, and then set up his own marshmallow stick. "That was a dynamite haunted house, boys. By my count we collected three bushel baskets of old paper and tin. A right good haul for one night."

He plopped down next to Charles. "It was fun, don't you think, Chuck? Most every pretty gal from school was there. They sure made a fuss over you." Bobby shifted his voice to a feminine falsetto, "'Lawd a' mercy, Charlie, what in the world happened?' 'Land sakes, can I get you a soda or somethin'?'"

Charles grunted affirmatively, although he'd surprised himself by not being particularly interested in the high school girls that hovered over him. He'd felt an annoying tug at his heart when Patsy had said she could tell that he was "all taken care of" with his "bevy of beauties," and left his side to oversee the bobbing-for-apples contest.

He stared into the campfire's flame and wondered at himself.

"Okeydokey," announced Bobby. "Time for ghost stories. Chuck, you must know some doozies from England. What about Bloody Mary, for instance? What was she all about, anyway?"

"Eeewwww," said Jamie. "Was she oozing guts like a zombie?"

"Maybe she was a vampire, and ripped people's throats up when she bit them," suggested Johnny hopefully.

Wesley jumped in to answer, and Charles, surprised by his little brother's sudden confidence, let him speak for them.

"No, she was a queen," said Wesley. "She was Catholic and hated Protestants. So she beheaded them or burned them at the stake if they wouldn't convert. Dreadful woman. So . . . Bloody Mary."

The boys stared at Wesley.

"Wait," Bobby shook his head in confusion. "Mary killed people just because they weren't Catholic? They were still English, right?"

"Right," said Wesley.

"They just worshipped the Lord in a different way from her?"

"Right," answered Wesley.

"That's wacky," said Ron.

"About as insane as refusing to invite a friend to a party just because his skin color is different," Wesley whispered to Charles.

Charles was relieved the Ratcliffs didn't hear that comment. He frowned at Wesley.

"What is it about religion that makes you people in Europe want to kill each other?" Bobby asked in earnestness. "You know, a few months back Mr. Epstein was worried sick over what's happening to the Jews there at the hands of the Nazis. Hitler's taken all their property and denied them their jobs and even herded them into walled-off sections of cities. Some just seem to disappear altogether. Mr. Epstein says the Allies have hardly paid any attention to it. He was real upset. You hear anything about stuff like that from home, Chuck?"

Before Charles could reply, Ron interrupted, pulling the attention back to himself. He was forever doing that when Charles and Bobby were talking to each other. "Hey, hey, I've got a good ghost story. There was this guy, see, asleep in his bedroom, snoring peaceful-like. Something woke him with a jolt. He sat up. He saw two tiny shiny eyes staring at him from the bottom of his bed. No matter how he shifted around, those eyes followed him. 'Go away,' he shouted, but the eyes just kind of danced around like they were laughing at him. So the man reached into the drawer of his nightstand. He pulled out his revolver. *BLAM!*" Ron stopped short.

Both twins flinched and gasped at the *BLAM*. "What happened next?" they squeaked.

"The next morning they found the man dead, swimming in his own blood."

"How?" breathed the twins. "Why?"

"He'd shot his own foot off!" Ron guffawed. "Those shiny eyes were his big ole toenails reflecting the moonlight."

"That's stupid," Bobby said, even though he laughed. "Okay, I see you're ready for ghost stories, so let me start. I've got a good one, a real sad, awful one, especially 'cause it's true. And it happened"—he lowered and lengthened his voice for effect—"right here, during the War between the States." He swept his hand out gesturing to the battlefield. "Ready?"

The boys nodded.

"Sooooo . . . As y'all know, the Battle of Malvern Hill was the last in the Seven Days campaign. If the Yankees captured Richmond, the war could have ended right then and there. If General Bobby Lee beat them bad enough, though, that might have ended the war, too. So each side was desperate to win the day.

"Right about here"—Bobby pointed to a stand of trees—"was a small group of Southerners, trying to hold their position. Over there"—Bobby pointed down the slope—"was an Irish brigade from the Union. Its captain saw that the Confederates were holding their ground because of the leadership of one daring boy. That Yankee officer called his best sharpshooter and told him he had to take that boy down.

"The sharpshooter raised his rifle and took aim, waiting until that brave Southern boy exposed himself again. Then he fired. *BANG!*"

All the brothers flinched.

"The boy fell over," Bobby continued. "His company scattered. The Union took the hill. Then the Yankee officer told the sharpshooter to go find the boy because he was so courageous he deserved to get medical help if he still lived.

"Well sir, by and by, the sharpshooter found the boy. He turned the Confederate over onto his back, face up. The boy opened his eyes for just a moment to look at the Yankee sharpshooter. He whispered, 'Father.' Then he died." Bobby paused dramatically, making sure he had his audience's full attention before delivering the climactic sentences of his story. His voice grew sad as he told it: "It was the sharpshooter's very own son, who'd run away to the South before the war. The sharpshooter had killed his own child, not recognizing him."

The boys gasped.

Bobby nodded solemnly. "That poor sharpshooter set off howling up the hill, calling for a charge, straight into a line of Confederates. It was total suicide—they riddled him with bullets." Bobby stopped once more. "People say on a still night, you hear the crackling shot of a rifle and then the most blood-curdling outcry of grief and regret you can imagine. If we sit here long enough"—Bobby lowered his voice to a whisper—"we might feel him pass right by us, a-wailing and a-carrying on, reminding us to think twice about going to war."

That silenced the boys.

Bobby gazed into the darkness and added in a voice hushed with thought, "Thousands of boys died here, and the battle didn't decide a thing. I swear, man is a perplexing species." He sighed. "You know, a bunch of the guys from last year's football squad are shipping out soon. Bet they're heading over for the coming invasion of France." He turned back to the campfire and poked at it with a stick before looking back up to his brothers.

The twins' eyes had expanded in fear to the size of golf balls.

"Oops," Bobby murmured, recognizing that his ghost story had probably been a bit too much for them. He clapped his hands, changing the mood abruptly. "Who can spit into the fire from ten feet out?"

Long into the night, as the other boys slept by the campfire, Charles stewed over that ghost story and Bobby's reaction to Bloody Mary. It was the first time he'd really thought about the ridiculousness of England's Catholics and Protestants murdering each other, basically over how they said their prayers. And what about the American Civil War? How could a father and son end up on opposite sides of such an argument?

Would adults ever stop slaughtering one another? Well, at least this world war was a righteous fight, Charles told himself. Hitler was a monster, no question about that. He had to be stopped. Of course, Hitler should have been shut down before he gained so much power. So many people, including the British—if he were honest about it—had looked the other way for so long, hoping that what was happening, really wasn't. And why hadn't some good Germans spoken up against the prejudices Hitler was spewing, even if all their friends and neighbors bought *der Führer*'s racist and anti-Semitic baloney?

That thought drew Charles up short.

He looked over at Wesley, who was flopping about on the ground, probably having nightmares again. He'd let his little brother down, hadn't he? Charles hadn't spoken up when Bobby said Freddy couldn't come to the party just because he was a Negro. He hadn't because he knew it was an accepted prejudice, just like the Brits' attitude about the natives of their colony India. Charles hadn't wanted to rock the boat.

Suddenly Charles felt ashamed.

Out in the night, a fox yelped, sounding alarmingly like a woman screaming. Wesley flipped over again and whimpered.

Charles got up and sat himself down by Wesley. He put his hand on top his brother's blond curls, just like their mother had done countless times during the night for Charles when he'd had bad dreams.

Wesley quieted, and slept. Under that big, open, starry American sky, Charles kept watch and thought of England and the changes the Allies themselves would have to make when they finally won the war.

15 November 1943

Dearest Mumsy,

Things are finally looking UP! I have a friend! His name is Freddy. He loves books nearly as much as I do. But he has hardly any, so I am lending him mine. He has started with Treasure Island. Now we have such fun talking PIRATES! Did you know there was a horrid pirate named Blackbeard who used the Outer Banks just south of here as his hideaway cove? Now the Yanks call it Torpedo Junction because of all the ships Hitler's U-boats sunk there last year. Some of my classmates go to those beaches, but I think I would rather not. Sometimes pieces of blown-up ships and dead sailors wash up.

School is better now that we are past the War of 1812 and focusing on Thanksgiving. At an assembly for the lower grades about the Pilgrims' feast with the Indians, I am to recite a Longfellow poem about Hiawatha. 'By the shores of GITCHE GUMEE' is how it begins. I do so love Indian words. They are ever so much more interesting sounding than our British names, and I think it is brilliant to call men 'braves' instead of 'boys' or 'lads.' I wish I could meet a REAL Indian, though, one wearing an eagle feather and carrying a tomahawk like Tonto.

I hope you are well. Are you safe?

Your loving son,
Wesley Bishop

Chapter Eleven

"Freddy knows how. Why can't you show me?"

"'Tisn't mine, Wes," Charles whispered irritably, holding a shotgun just out of his little brother's reach. "That's why."

They stood in the back porch mudroom with the Ratcliff boys, pulling on their coats and boots at five A.M. Despite the early hour, the boys chattered happily about going hunting. Mr. Ratcliff was letting them make some pocket money by hunting wild turkeys and quail off Curles Neck to sell for Thanksgiving dinners. Most Richmond city residents wouldn't be able to find traditional turkey to buy because farm-raised domestic ones were mostly being sent to troops overseas or on military bases in the United States. The Ratcliffs had a good stash of birdshot left even though shotgun shells were rationed. Mr. Ratcliff was a crack shot, able to take down crows sitting in trees with a .22 rifle. So the boys were hoping to make a bundle of cash to use for buying Christmas presents for one another.

The twins were chanting, “Turkey, turkey.” They didn’t seem to mind that they and Wesley had been relegated to manning the dogs and carrying the kill.

Wesley, on the other hand, was mortified to be lumped in with seven-year-olds. “I’m big enough to hold a shotgun, you know,” Wesley whispered back.

“Look, Wes, a gun is dangerous,” Charles answered. “You shouldn’t handle it unless you’ve been taught. Like Bobby’s taught me.”

Despite their lowered voices, Ron overheard. “It’s not like your stupid set of toy six-shooters, old chum,” he sniped. “What’s that game you still play? Cowboys and Indians?”

The twins stopped chanting. Johnny looked like he actually might be interested in a Wild West game. But Jamie mimicked Ron’s sneer.

Wesley felt his face flame up in embarrassment. Charles sighed. Wesley knew what Charles’s raised eyebrows meant: *Come on, Wes, stand up for yourself so I don’t have to this time.*

But Mrs. Ratcliff interrupted the tense moment. “Boys,” she called from the kitchen, “come get your bag lunches. Don’t want to get hungry out there on Turkey Bend, do you?”

Propping their guns beside the screened door, Bobby, Charles, and Ron shooed the twins inside and entered the kitchen behind them. Wesley lingered. He couldn’t help himself. He reached out and picked up the shotgun Bobby had lent Charles.

It was heavy and cold, just a foot shy of being as tall as he was. Wesley hoisted the gun, resting the wooden butt against his shoulder. He struggled to balance it, gripping the well-oiled wooden body that supported the long steel barrel. The steel ring that encircled the trigger was oddly elegant and beckoned Wesley to wrap his fingers through it. He looked into the gun's small sight. Imagining he was a movie cowboy hiding in rocks from marauding Apaches, Wesley slowly pulled back the gun's hammer as if ready to shoot.

Oh, right, better make sure the safety latch is on, Wesley cautioned himself. Still holding the gun up—aimed, cocked, and ready to fire, with his finger on the trigger—he slid his thumb up and down until it found the small safety lever. Not really knowing which direction was on, which off, he pushed it. As he did, he bobbled the gun a bit, his finger tightening on the trigger.

KABLAM!

The shotgun roared. The kickback threw Wesley backward against the wall.

"Gawd Almighty!"

"What the blazes?"

"Hell's bells!"

Shouting, the Ratcliffs crowded into the room that for Wesley was swimming with stars. He rubbed the back of his head and tried to focus. Mostly he saw knees. Then Wesley looked up and realized the shotgun explosion had blasted a hole right through the screened door. "Oh no!" he cried.

Everyone seemed to talk at the same time.

"What a dope!" said Ron.

"Lord a' mercy," cried Mrs. Ratcliff. "That could have gone through the wall into the kitchen."

"Are you all right, honey?" Patsy asked.

"Bloody hell!" Charles grabbed his brother, pulled him to his feet, and patted him up and down, searching for bullet holes. He exhaled with relief and for a split second he and Wesley smiled at each other. Then Charles's attitude turned furious. He shook Wesley by his collar. "Didn't I tell you not to touch the gun?"

"Hold on a minute, Chuck. Give him some air." Mr. Ratcliff reached out and propped Wesley up. "Mary Lee, look at his eyes. Seem kind of crossed to me. Think the boy's all right?"

Mrs. Ratcliff checked his arms and hands, assessed his face again, and then patted it gently. "He's fine, just shaken up a mite." She smiled at Wesley. "Would have hated to send you home in a box, sugar."

"We best get going, then. Time's a-wasting." Mr. Ratcliff leaned over and picked up the shotgun. "Good thing it wasn't a double-barrel," he joked.

"What? That's all you're going to say?" Ron pointed at the hole in the screened door. "That will cost a pretty penny to fix, Dad."

"Hush up, Ron," Bobby snapped.

Mr. Ratcliff examined the door. "I have more screening in the shed. We can repair that wood and paint it. Considering what could have happened there's not much damage done. Give you a chance to practice your carpentry skills, Ron."

"But... But..." Ron sputtered.

"Son, I saw many a boy—gentle ones, bookish ones like Wesley here—make the exact same mistake in the Great War. They just shouldn't have been around guns to begin with. However, I do, as a matter of fact, have more to say."

Mr. Ratcliff turned to the two oldest boys. “Why was that gun loaded in the house? Chuck, isn’t that the gun we gave you to use?”

Charles’s mouth dropped open and his face flushed red. “I. . . I. . .”

“It’s my fault, sir,” Bobby spoke up. “I loaded it to show Chuck how. I wasn’t thinking.”

It was a lie—a wonderful, selfless lie for friendship. It’s why Wesley and all the boys admired Bobby so much. But Charles wouldn’t let Bobby take the fall for him. “Bobby is trying to cover for me, Mr. Ratcliff. I did it myself.”

“Humph.” Mr. Ratcliff considered the pair a moment. “You know a loaded gun in the house is dangerous? And plain old stupid?”

The two boys nodded.

“You’re the oldest. I count on you two to be sensible, to set an example for the younger ones.”

The boys nodded.

“Never do that again.”

“We won’t, sir,” Charles and Bobby replied in unison.

“See that you don’t,” he finished sternly. “Let’s go. We’re going to miss our gobblers if we don’t hurry.”

As the boys piled into the truck’s flatbed, neither Charles nor Bobby would look at or speak to their younger brothers.

Mr. Ratcliff drove fast toward Curles Neck and the oxbow loop the river made around Turkey Island. The road’s speed limit had been lowered to thirty-five miles per hour to conserve gas, but he pushed the rattletrap truck faster. It was critical for them to be in position before complete daybreak, when the turkeys could see them and flee.

Wesley hunkered down against the cold wind. The two setters, Flynn and Buster, lay down beside him, as if they anticipated the day's plan. The Ratcliffs would hunt turkey in the morning and quail in the late afternoon. Wesley was to keep the dogs quiet during the turkey hunt, then help them track quail later.

"Well, if I'm in the doghouse," he whispered to them, "you're good company." Wesley stroked the dogs' heads and watched the landscape whiz by. Raised in the crowded, bricked streets of London with its miniature, manicured flower-box gardens, Wesley was still entranced by the wild, overgrown beauty of Tidewater Virginia.

Tall trees stretched over the road to just barely touch one another, like the fingertips of dancers. In the summer, they made a wondrous choreography of swaying, light-dappled green. That early morning, however, only a few oaks clung to their autumn-brown leaves. The carrot-colored maples, golden hickories, and crimson dogwood had already shed most of theirs in windswept pirouettes of color.

Now the bare trees created a bleak latticework of black branches over the road. Wesley shivered and looked away to the roadside as the truck hurried past a bog with broken tree trunks rising out of it like rotted teeth. In warm months, those mini-swamps teemed with wild blue irises and pink water lilies, dragonflies and green turtles basking in sunlight along sticks protruding from the water. Now the bogs, like the trees, were barren nightmare material. They gave Wesley the creeps.

He'd be glad when the sun came up.

Mr. Ratcliff turned off the road and shifted into neutral to let the truck coast silently to a halt. There was the slimmest shard of golden light low on the horizon. Quickly and quietly, everyone scampered to the ground, pushing the doors closed to avoid giveaway slams. They were heading for a thick stand of oak trees Bobby had scouted the previous week. A large flock of turkeys was roosting in the gnarly trees at night, then eating fallen acorns in the early morning before moving to fields to look for insects. Bobby had explained to Wesley and Charles that it would be far easier to shoot the turkeys before they reached open ground, where the birds could run as fast as twenty-five miles per hour or fly away.

"Don't let those dogs bark," Mr. Ratcliff whispered to Wesley as he, Bobby, and Ron turned to tiptoe into the woods, trailed by the twins carrying burlap sacks.

"Try not to make a fool of yourself again," Charles added before following Bobby into the darkness.

Keeping two good hunting dogs quiet in woods salted with all sorts of animal scents was not easy. Wesley clung to their collars to keep them from leaping out of the flatbed to follow the Ratcliffs.

"I can't help it, boys," he told them. He broke off the crusts of his PB&J sandwich to reward them for staying still. Wesley had seen foxhounds in the English countryside when his family went on holiday, but he knew very little about hunting dogs until coming to the States. Flynn and Buster were working dogs, trained to sniff out quail. But they never rushed in once they found their prey, no matter how much they trembled with excitement. They'd freeze, front paw lifted, their nose pointed straight toward the birds to show their human master where his quarry was. The hunter would scare the quails into flight, shooting them in the air. Only then would the dogs rush forward to find the fallen birds and carry them gently back, dropping them at their master's feet as other dogs might a ball, hoping for a game of fetch.

Trying to adopt their self-discipline, Wesley sat quietly, listening to the woods wake up. Leaves rustled as squirrels busied themselves collecting their final treasures for winter. *Wheat-eater-wheat-eater-wheat*, Carolina wrens called back and forth. A pileated woodpecker hammered a tree trunk. Landing on the truck's roof, a cardinal cocked its head to eye Wesley and then flitted away, alarmed, *chip-chip-chip-chip*ping to warn his mate of intruders.

Finally, he just had to stretch, so Wesley hopped off the truck. He and the dogs headed for the woods in the opposite direction from where the Ratcliffs had disappeared. As they padded through the forest, Buster and Flynn suddenly pricked up their ears. Wesley strained to hear what they did.

From a long way away a sharp whistle cut through the air: *Quail-lee, quail-lee.*

Quail! The birds were calling to one another to group in a covey for the morning.

The dogs whined and looked expectantly at Wesley as if to say, *You stupid bloke, let us do our jobs.*

"We're supposed to stay here, boys," he reasoned with them.

But the dogs quivered in anticipation of a hunt.

Quail-lee.

Wesley knew the call meant quail were gathering to search the field for seed. By midday the quail would fall silent and head back into the forest's brambles, in a feeding pattern that was the exact opposite of turkeys'. The quail wouldn't call to one another again like this—making it easier for the Ratcliffs to find them—until evening. Maybe Wesley could make up for his shotgun gaffe by locating the covey now and saving Mr. Ratcliff the time of searching them out later.

"Come on, boys." Wesley struck out, following the quail's morning revelry.

Quail-lee.

Wesley waded through briars and pushed past dangling grapevines to emerge onto a wide field tangled with dried-out wildflowers, tall grasses, and thistles.

Quail-lee.

The dogs plunged into the grasses. Wesley waded after them.

Quail-lee.

The call was farther away now. Maybe his thrashing through the field had scared off the quail. He stopped. Bobby and the brothers could actually call back and forth with quail, especially in the spring when the males looked for mates, whistling *bob-white, bob-bob-white.* This autumn call was harder to imitate, the first part high and long, lifting and falling in pitch, the second lower and short, anxious-sounding.

He whistled.

After a moment, a quail called back. *Quail-lee.* And then another. *Quail-lee.*

Wesley smiled, thrilled to be talking with birds. "Just like Doctor Dolittle," he whispered to Buster and Flynn, who had now slowed to a stealthy creep.

The calls became closer and closer, seeming to surround him. Wesley had to be conversing with at least a dozen quail now. They were definitely converging on him. He tried not to think about the fact that the gentle little brown birds with their delicate white markings were destined for a Thanksgiving dinner table.

He'd been paralleling Turkey Island Creek. Now ahead of him, shimmering in silver reflections of the low rising sun was the James River oxbow. He paused to watch an eagle lift off from a tall snag on the riverbank and torque its white tail like a rudder to navigate the winds. So strange that both the Americans and the Nazis had the eagle for their symbol, he mused.

Quail-lee.

Wesley frowned. That call was really close. And funny-sounding. Wispy, not sharp and clean like the birds'. More like . . . like a human imitation.

Before Wesley could realize the danger he was in, he heard a rushing through the grasses and, in a flurry of panicked flapping, two dozen quail surged into the air right in front of him.

KABLAM! KABLAM!

Dead birds showered down around him.

Terrified, Wesley stumbled backward. He clutched his left arm where he felt a sudden horrendous burning. He tripped and landed on his back, whacking his head, hard. He reached up to hold his throbbing skull, and Wesley realized his fingertips were bloody.

"Good God," he cried, as a whirling sickness overcame him. "I've been shot!"

Then he felt nothing.

Chapter Twelve

"Here," said a commanding voice. "Drink this."

Wesley felt a cold tin cup pressed to his mouth, then a metallic-tasting liquid stung his tongue and throat. He coughed, his eyes popping open.

"That's better."

"Where am I?" Wesley tried to focus. He was laid out on a blanket near a low campfire, thick with embers. An old man knelt beside him, holding the cup and a bottle of something golden.

"In my hunting camp."

Wesley sat up and looked around. There were Flynn and Buster, happily chewing on bones, lying beside another dog. On a lean-to shed hung a dozen shot quail. He could hear water gently lapping against shoreline nearby. The sun was now bright and warm against his face. And whatever that liquid was had burned his insides warm, too.

"What happened?"

"You stepped into my line of fire. The sun was rising and in my eyes. I didn't see you."

"What?" Wesley was so confused. Then he noticed another burning sensation and reached for his left arm. It was bandaged tightly above his elbow.

"Some birdshot winged you," the man explained. "Just scratches. I've cleaned them. You are lucky it wasn't more."

"Wait a minute," said Wesley, beginning to remember. "You shot me?"

"Yes," the man answered, sitting back on his heels.

Wesley stared, for the first time noticing how different the man looked. He was deeply tanned, with high, pronounced cheekbones and a large, long nose. His graying hair was black and straight, cut blunt, hanging just below his ears. His eyes were large, a black-brown, and almond shaped. It was a rugged, slightly exotic face.

Wesley gasped with a thought. Recently the navy had displayed a captured Japanese submarine in Norfolk, and the Ratcliffs had gone to see it. This man looked a tiny bit like the photographs of Japanese officers displayed on the wharf near the sub.

"Are you . . ." Wesley lowered his voice to a nervous whisper. "Are you a Japanese sailor on the run?"

The man burst out laughing. "No."

Befuddled, Wesley murmured, "But you're not Negro like Freddy."

"No."

Wesley kept searching his mind for the image that matched this man. "Wait!" He gasped again. "Are you—oh my!—are you an Indian?"

The man smiled. "I am Chickahominy."

Wesley couldn't believe it. He was actually, finally, in the presence of a real live Indian! He sat up and raised his hand in salute. "How!"

"How what?"

"That's what Indians say, isn't it?"

The man laughed again. "Only in Hollywood. I should introduce myself. My name is Paul Johns." He bowed his head. "And I must apologize for shooting you."

"Oh, that's all right." Birdshot was a small price to pay to meet a real live Indian! "Do you live near here?"

"Not far."

"In a tepee?"

"No," the man answered with a patient smile. "In a regular house, like yours, with a vegetable garden and flowerbeds. Besides, my people never lived in tepees. We lived in long houses, made from trees and bark."

"Oh, I would have loved to have seen one."

"Me too," said the man. "Where are you from, son, that you ask all these questions?"

"From England."

"Ah." The man nodded. "That's the accent. Then you are one of them."

"Them?"

"Them that began our ruin. Thanksgiving is coming, right?

Well, we have a different perspective on the holiday. My people taught you about corn and tobacco. You English brought disease and stole our lands."

Now Wesley frowned. He hadn't ever thought of that, just about Captain Smith's dashing explorations and the romance between Pocahontas and John Rolfe. He changed the subject. "What's that?" He pointed to a large ivory-colored disk hanging around the man's throat. It was the size of a teacup saucer, and its center was pinched, making it look like a dragon's scale.

"This?" the man reached for his necklace. "It's a boney plate from the back of a sturgeon, the giant ocean fish that swims up the James to spawn. This came from one that was eight feet long."

"For real? I've never seen one," Wesley said.

"Come spring you may see one leap out of the water and shake itself in the air, before landing with a crash. They say long ago our young warriors proved their manhood by setting nets and then wrestling the sturgeon until they wore out."

Wesley's eyes grew round. "Did you do that?"

Once more the man laughed. "No. But I've caught a few sturgeons in my life. Would you like a boney plate for your own?"

"Yes, please!" said Wesley.

The man walked toward the water's edge. Wesley followed and spotted a duck blind and a canoe tied up in a labyrinth of marsh grasses. "Oh, oh, oh! Is that canoe yours?"

"Do you always ask this many questions?"

Wesley blushed and stopped himself from asking why it

was an ordinary-looking canvas boat and not a dug-out log like he'd seen in books.

"Let me ask you a few," countered the man. "What are you doing out alone with hunting dogs but no gun, flushing a covey of quail?"

Wesley explained.

Suddenly, the man seemed uneasy. "You need to go back. They'll be worried about you." He sifted through a large pile of empty oyster shells and fished out a sturgeon plate to hand Wesley. It was thick and hard, like a piece of a knight's armor.

"Blimey! Thanks, Mr. Johns. I can't wait to show my brother."

"Since you are so interested in my people," the man said, "let's pretend we are making a peace pact—like Powhatan and Captain Smith. Instead of smoking a peace pipe like in the movies, I'll give you this sturgeon bone and some of the quail you flushed out."

"Oh yes, please. Thank you ever so much."

The man walked back to his campfire and put six quail in a bag. He held the bag just out of Wesley's reach as he said, "And you won't call the sheriff, will you?"

"Why would I do that?"

"Not everyone around here feels as you do about native peoples. Some folks might take a Chickahominy winging a white child in a hunting accident as proof that we, as a people, are careless and dangerous. Do you understand?"

Wesley didn't, but he said, "I won't tell. I promise. My arm feels fine."

"Then we have our peace pact," the man said with a smile.

"Come back this spring with your brother. I will take you two out in my canoe to see the sturgeon."

Later that day, when the Ratcliffs came out of the woods, carrying five large turkeys, Wesley explained that he'd been walking the dogs and accidentally flushed out quail that a hunter shot and then shared with him. He didn't mention getting peppered himself. The sun was setting, and in the gloom no one noticed the tear in his jacket. Plus the Ratcliffs were tired and ready to go home, perfectly happy to accept a bag full of quail already provided. They didn't ask questions.

Only to Charles did Wesley show the sturgeon plate. Excitedly, he explained that Paul Johns was Chickahominy and had promised to take them out in his canoe to look for sturgeon. "He's a real live Indian," Wesley whispered excitedly. "But you can't snitch, Charles. I promised him."

"I won't," Charles answered stoutly. "Did you say a canoe?"

Charles listened carefully as Wesley described the canoe and how Paul Johns had tied it up in the marsh. "I've never seen a canoe myself," he commented thoughtfully. "Did it look seaworthy?"

"Oh my goodness, rather," answered Wesley. "Why do you ask?"

"Well, because. . . ." Charles rubbed his chin. "What would I tell our father if I let you go out on some rickety canoe that got in trouble?"

"No worries there, Charles! It was tip-top!"

"Hmmmm," Charles murmured, then abruptly changed the subject. "Want to hear 'bout the turkey shoot?

"Oh yes!" Wesley answered.

Charles described it in such gory detail, Wesley was sorry he asked.

1 December 1943

Dear Dad,

It is strange to say this so far ahead of time but Happy Christmas! The Yanks are now letting people ship five-pound packages, so Wes and I hope our presents make it to you. If no one nips anything you should receive: soap, matches, writing paper, typewriter ribbons, and coffee. We know it is nearly impossible to get any of that back home these days.

Coffee is not tea, of course, but it is released from rationing because South American cargo boats are making the run into Norfolk regularly again since the Yanks are doing better at finding old Adolf's U-boats. Wish we could get you some of the bananas they bring.

I have also included a very droll American novel I read in school—Adventures of Huckleberry Finn by Mark Twain. Do not tell Master Whitten I say so, but it is far more interesting than Trollope. The Negro dialect might be hard going for you, but it is quite poetic when you get the hang of it. Twain's depiction of the Mississippi River is wonderful. It will give you a slight idea of what the James River is like, although unlike the Mississippi, the currents shift every six hours or so.

I see now why you always say that geography can affect the mindset of a man. I must say I feel the pull of the James to the sea. It must have been the way the Thames worked on Sir Walter Raleigh to send him here so long ago.

We just had Thanksgiving. I actually 'bagged' the turkey we had for the holiday dinner. Bobby taught me to shoot. So now I can help the Ratcliffs 'bring home the bacon' when they hunt. Plus, I shall be prepared to shoot at the Jerries—hint, hint.

I will miss our annual feast of Christmas leftovers and bubble and squeak on Boxing Day. Wes was so young when we left he does not even remember Boxing Day, which I think sad. Here's to our seeing one another in the New Year.

Yours, Charles

Chapter Thirteen

"Wesley," Patsy called up the stairs, "can you come help crack these walnuts, please?"

Reluctantly, Wesley closed his book. He'd been completely absorbed reading about Sitting Bull and the Sioux.

Charles looked up from his chemistry notes. He knew he should stay put, but downstairs there was a warm fireplace and company and plenty of ways to avoid molecular formulas. "I'm coming too," he announced. "It's almost time for the CBS news roundup."

They stormed the stairs together.

On the first floor, the house was filled with the scent of buttery biscuit dough rising in a bowl atop a radiator for the next morning. Mrs. Ratcliff hummed in the kitchen, cleaning up dinner dishes. Mr. Ratcliff sat in his wingback armchair by the fireplace reading the *Richmond News-Leader.* At his feet, the twins played war, grabbing cards back and forth from each other.

"Looks like Santa Claus will be coming to Miller and Rhodes this year after all, boys," he said to them as he turned a page.

"Goody!"

"What are you hoping Father Christmas will bring you?" Wesley asked as he flopped down on the couch beside Patsy. Balanced on her lap was a huge bowl of walnuts the boys had gathered from the yard for Mrs. Ratcliff to use in the apple-walnut bread she baked for Christmas presents. Patsy threw her hands over it to keep Wesley's flop from sending the walnuts flying.

"That new board game Chutes and Ladders." "No, Uncle Wiggily." The boys bickered.

Charles had seen Patsy sitting on the sofa's flowery chintz slipcovers a thousand times and never thought much about her appearance. But something about that night drew him up short, the glow of the firelight on her face maybe. She looks like a human blossom, he mused, sitting on a cloth garden. *Oh for pity's sake!* Charles gagged on his icky-sweet simile. *What a besotted dope!*

Patsy noticed him staring at her. She frowned, glanced down at the bowl, then at her dress and collar, as if checking to make sure she hadn't spilled dinner all over herself or something, which would explain Charles's looking at her that way.

She'd caught him! Charles cleared his throat and stretched, then pretended to check for lint on the back of the couch.

Patsy cocked her head quizzically as she asked, "Don't you need to study for that test you were telling me about, Chuck?"

"Naw. It's in the bag, no sweat."

"Really? I wouldn't have passed chemistry without Henry tutoring me."

Charles knew Patsy didn't care for science. Her favorite classes were English and art. In fact, she was an amazing sketch artist. She kept a notebook full of her own drawings—of songbirds, wildflowers, her mother ironing, the twins paying hide-and-seek. He'd seen her slam it shut when her brothers came near. Curious, he'd snuck a look. She was really talented. But he never said anything, since she seemed shy about them.

Charles started to admit that he, too, wasn't that good at science, that his strengths were sports and political history. But he knew Americans seemed to expect boys to love math and science and want to be engineers or builders of some kind. He didn't want to seem like he didn't fit the proper male mold.

So he changed the subject instead. "May I turn on the news, Mr. Ratcliff?"

"Sure thing, Chuck." Mr. Ratcliff checked his watch. "I'm glad you kept track of the hour. I would have missed it reading up on Christmas happenings." Mr. Ratcliff closed his newspaper and picked up his pipe, stuffing it with loose tobacco before lighting it. "About time you two went to bed," he said to the twins.

"No, Daddy! We want to hear the radio too!" they chimed as Charles turned the radio's knob on with a loud *click*.

From the wooden, Cathedral-arched box a crackly voice announced: "CBS World News now brings you a special broadcast from London. Columbia's correspondent, Edward R. Murrow, was on one of the RAF bombing planes that smashed at Berlin last night, in one of the heaviest attacks of the war. Forty-one bombers were lost in the raid and three out of the five correspondents who flew with the raiders failed to return."

With that, worries over bedtime stopped. Patsy froze, nutcracker in hand. Everyone shushed one another to listen.

Charles crowded onto the sofa beside Patsy and Wesley, and leaned forward to concentrate on the report.

"This is London," Murrow began, in a deep voice that resonated over the static and feedback whistle of a transatlantic broadcast. "Last night, some of the young gentlemen of the RAF took me to Berlin."

"As far as Berlin—think of that," said Mr. Ratcliff, puffing, smoke swirling around him.

"All I can think about, Daddy," Patsy countered, "is that forty-one planes didn't make it back. Forty-one. That's four hundred and ten boys, isn't it?"

Charles nodded.

Murrow set the stage—telling that his pilot's name was Jock, that he was the squadron leader, and that the big, black, four-motored Lancaster plane he flew was named *D for Dog*. Right before takeoff, Murrow added, a small station wagon delivered a thermos of coffee, chewing gum, an orange, and a bit of chocolate to each crew member.

Pulled in by Murrow's voice, Mrs. Ratcliff entered from the kitchen. "Poor lambs," she murmured. "Only that to eat during a whole night of flying?"

"Shhhhhhh."

Bobby drifted into the room now too, a trigonometry textbook in hand, as Murrow described the takeoff. The Lancaster planes—"Lancs," Murrow called them—climbed "for the place where men must burn oxygen to live."

Patsy put down the nutcracker. Charles noticed her hands had started to tremble.

"Soon we were out over the North Sea," Murrow continued. "Buzz, the bomb aimer, crackled through . . . 'There's a battle going on the starboard beam.' We couldn't see the aircraft, but we could see the jets of red tracer being exchanged."

"Why couldn't they see the aircraft?" whispered Johnny.

"You Yanks fly daylight missions, but we Brits follow up at night. Mr. Murrow is describing a British flight," answered Charles. "So it's dark except for the explosions."

"Shhhhhhh."

Ron stood in the doorway now, leaning against the frame.

Murrow's voice went on describing one dangerous moment after another on the hard-fought journey to the bomb target: "There was a burst of yellow flame and Jock remarked, 'That's a fighter going down.' . . . Suddenly those dirty gray clouds turned white and we were over the outer searchlight defenses . . . *D-Dog* seemed like a black bug on a white sheet. The flak began coming up. . . .

"By this time we were about thirty miles from our target area in Berlin." Murrow paused for emphasis. "That thirty miles was the longest flight I have ever made."

"I bet," Charles muttered.

"Flares were sprouting all over the sky," Murrow continued, "reds and greens and yellows, and we were flying straight for the center of the fireworks. . . . Off to the starboard a Lanc was caught by at least fourteen searchlight beams. We could see him twist and turn and finally break out."

The cadence of Murrow's voice sped up as he described the Nazi searchlights finding and holding individual planes in cone-like beams so the Luftwaffe fighters could see and home in on them. "Another Lanc was coned on our starboard beam. . . . The German fighters were at him.

"And then, with no warning at all, *D-Dog* was filled with an unhealthy white light. . . . Jock's quiet Scots voice beat into my ears, 'Steady, lads, we've been coned.'"

Patsy gasped.

"Jock's slender body lifted half out of the seat as he jammed the control column forward and to the left. We were going down. Jock was wearing woolen gloves with the fingers cut off. I could see his fingernails turn white as he gripped the wheel. And then I was on my knees, flat on the deck, for he had whipped the *Dog* back into a climbing turn."

"It's okay," Charles reached out and patted Patsy's hand. "They fly evasively like that to get out of the searchlights." The pain in Patsy's eyes hurt him.

"*D-Dog* was corkscrewing. As we rolled down on the other side, I began to see what was happening to Berlin. . . . The bombers' small incendiaries were going down like a fistful of white rice . . . glowing white and then turning red. The cookies, the four-thousand-pound high explosives, were bursting below like great sunflowers gone mad. And then, as we started down again, still held in the lights, I remembered that the *Dog* still had one of those cookies and a whole basket of incendiaries in his belly.

"And the lights still held us." Murrow paused, then added, "And I was very frightened."

Charles looked down with surprise as Johnny scooched across the floor to lean up against his and Wesley's legs, like a puppy seeking comfort.

"Finally," Murrow continued, "we were out of the cone, flying level."

"Thank the Lord," murmured Mrs. Ratcliff.

"Shhhhhhhh," everyone shushed her.

"I looked down," announced Murrow, "and the white fires had turned red. They were beginning to merge and spread, just like butter does on a hot plate. . . . The bomb doors were opened. . . . There was a gentle, confident upward thrust under my feet . . . The incendiaries went, and *D-Dog* seemed lighter and easier to handle."

Relieved, the Ratcliffs shifted in their seats.

But Murrow's mission was far from over: "I began to breathe . . . when there was a tremendous *whoomph*, an unintelligible shout from the tail gunner, and *D-Dog* shivered and lost altitude. I looked to the port side and there was a Lancaster that seemed close enough to touch. He had whipped straight under us—missed us by twenty-five, fifty feet. . . .”

“What an idiot that pilot must be,” Ron sniped.

“Shut up, Ron,” Bobby spoke before Charles could. “Do you know how hard it must be for them to not crash into one another, flying in such tight formations, in the dark, and trying to dodge flak and fighters?”

“Shhhhhhh!”

Murrow was still talking. “Jock was doing what I had heard him tell his pilots to do so often—flying dead on course. He flew straight into a huge green searchlight and, as he rammed the throttles home, remarked, ‘We’ll have a little trouble getting away from this one.’. . . The flak began coming up at us . . . winking off both wings. . . . A great orange blob of flak smacked up straight in front of us, and Jock . . . began to throw *D for Dog* up, around, and about again. When we were clear of the barrage, I asked him how close the bursts were and he said, ‘Not very close. When they’re really near, you can smell ’em.’”

Murrow paused again to admit, “That proved nothing, for I’d been holding my breath.”

The Ratcliffs let out their own breaths in unison.

Murrow told more about the homeward flight and then concluded about the raid: “Berlin was a kind of orchestrated hell—a terrible symphony of light and flame. . . . Men die in the sky while others are roasted alive in their cellars. . . . Right now the mechanics are probably working on *D-Dog*, getting him ready to fly"—Murrow paused one last time to drive home the point—"again."

Riveted by Murrow's grisly poetry, his depiction of the dangers the aircrew faced, they all remained absolutely still for several moments.

Finally, Charles dared to look at Patsy. Tears were sliding down her face, but her expression was defiant. "That settles it," she said, breaking the silence. "That could be Henry up there in *D for Dog*. That's what he has to endure. I'm not about to sit around and not do anything to help our fight."

She stood. "Daddy, I ran into Mr. Ewell at the library the other day. He's been volunteering as a plane spotter for the Aircraft Warning Service, but he's been called up by the army. He asked me to replace him. He gave me the handbook and the flashcards so I can memorize the planes I'll need to know. All I'll be doing is standing on the tower and watching the sky. Then I telephone the civilian defense office to report any aircraft I spot and which direction it's flying. It won't keep me from finishing my homework."

"Now hold on, girl. Wasn't Ewell doing that at night?"

"Just from four to nine o'clock, Daddy."

"It'll be dark when you have to walk home along the road." Mr. Ratcliff shook his head. "No."

Charles stood up too. "I'll go with her, Mr. Ratcliff. I wouldn't mind memorizing those planes myself. Could come in handy when I return to London. Frankly, sir, some older lads from my school are now RAF pilots. They might have been flying in that very raid Mr. Murrow described. I've got to start doing something myself."

Mr. Ratcliff frowned. "It's December. You'll freeze."

Now Mrs. Ratcliff stood. She smiled at her husband. "I'll send them off with extra coats and a thermos of hot chocolate, just like those boys in those planes. It'll be all right, Andy. They need to do this." She nodded her head toward Patsy and Charles and added gently. "Take a look, honey."

Mr. Ratcliff opened his mouth to argue some other point. But just as he did, Bing Crosby's newest song lilted out of the radio: *"I'll be home for Christmas. . . ."*

Charles caught his breath, furious at how the bittersweet song made his throat close up and his eyes burn. He put his hand on Wesley's shoulder and tightened his grip a bit, knowing Wesley would be feeling the same pangs he was. He willed himself to seem manly in front of the Ratcliffs.

For a moment Charles and Mr. Ratcliff gazed at each other as Crosby crooned on about making it home to family for Christmas.

"If only in my dreams." Crosby's voice trailed off.

Wesley sniffed.

"All right, Chuck." Mr. Ratcliff relented.

It was the best Christmas present Charles could have.

22 January 1944

Dearest Mum,

It was a terrific Christmas, except for not seeing you, of course. We even had a proper snowfall on the 28th with FIVE INCHES of good packing snow for snowballs and snowmen. Freddy and I built a fort with escape tunnels. It was brilliant! Even the brothers said so.

The Ratcliffs were awfully kind to us this Christmas. I am far too grown up now for toys, so the Ratcliffs gave me The Flickering Torch Mystery. It is the 22nd book in the Hardy Boys series. It is a cracking good mystery—about rare silkworms disappearing from a scientific research farm. Mrs Ratcliff said it was time I read some American books. I have nearly worn out the ones I brought from home. I hope you will not mind, I gave Freddy my copy of The Jungle Book for Christmas. He has no books of his own except some Uncle Wiggily adventures with the covers falling off that a lady from the Salvation Army gave him.

For Christmas, Patsy took us to see Lassie Come Home. Have you seen it? It is set in Yorkshire and stars a pretty little English girl named Elizabeth Taylor. (She is an evacuee, too!) Hearing all those British accents did make me rather homesick. Lassie is sold because her family is too poor to keep her. But she makes her way back to them through TERRIBLE danger all the way from Scotland. Charles got rather funny about it and wouldn't talk for the rest of the night.

Do you know there was a group of GERMAN POWs in the cinema? We spotted them as we left. Bobby had to hold on to Charles to keep him from shouting at them. I thought it frightfully strange. Freddy is not allowed in the movie house because he is a Negro. But they let in the Axis?

Oh, here is a news flash: In February, I get to go with Freddy to watch the launching of the aircraft carrier his daddy has been working on. Please stay safe and tell Hamlet he is as good as any old movie dog.

Your loving son,
Wesley Bishop

Dear Dad,

Happy New Year! I have made all sorts of resolutions for 1944. One is I shall never make fun of farmers again. I have certainly learned how hard their lot is, particularly in bad weather. We had sleet on Christmas Day and then a heavy snowfall three days later. The pipes in the barn's well froze and burst. I must have hauled a thousand pails of water from the creek for the chickens and the mules until we got it fixed. We had to shovel trails to the sheds. There was no just slogging through. Half the orchard trees split from the weight of the ice and snow. Mrs Ratcliff cried when she realised they would only get half the number of apples and damsons in the next few years as a result.

I have started plane-watching with Patsy for the Yanks' warning system. We stand in a tower and scan the sky with binoculars. Whenever we spot a plane, we dial up Civilian Defense and report what type and where it is headed. We have memorized the silhouettes of 54 planes, their markings, the number and placement of engines, the shape of their noses and tails, that sort of thing. I can now ID German and Japanese planes from a long distance, but we have only seen American aircraft, of course. There are more planes overhead here than you might think. The Richmond Air Base is only five miles away. We see them all the time at the farm. The trainees tend to return up the James and take a right turn over Curles Neck to approach the base for landing.

Identifying planes does make me feel like I am doing <u>something</u> for the war effort. But it is a joke compared to what I know the London skies have been filled with. The air force dropped sacks of flour on Richmond in a mock air raid to show what incendiary bombs could do. But splattered flour is not exactly a good replica of the flames of a firebomb. My mates would fall over laughing at the idea.

Did you make any resolutions for yourselves? I hope you have made one to let me come home this year. The Allies landed at Anzio today. Surely now we shall be able to beat back the Nazis in Italy, and then Hitler will have to shift his attention from bombing England to covering his own bum.

Keep safe and stay well.

Yours ever,
Charles

Chapter Fourteen

"Jiminy Cricket! Just like Daddy said!" Freddy crowed.

Wesley looked up and up and up at the gray sides of the USS *Ticonderoga*, docked within a massive labyrinth of scaffolding. He whistled. "Blimey! How big is that thing?"

Freddy grinned and recited the stats from memory: "Eight hundred, eighty-eight feet long, the length of two and a half football fields. It has eight boilers and four steam turbines. It'll carry eighty-two planes and three thousand, four hundred and forty-eight men. And," he added proudly, "my daddy helped build it."

"He sure did," said Alma, patting Freddy's arm. "It's the sixth aircraft carrier your daddy has helped build in Newport News in two years." She and Ed stood behind the boys, their hands resting on Wesley's and Freddy's shoulders to shield them from the push and shove of high-ranking dignitaries hurrying closer to the grandstand—a steady tide of naval officers in dress uniform, politicians in felt fedoras and heavy overcoats, and women in pearls, mink coats, white gloves, and Sunday-best hats.

"Thirty-four hundred men? That's a city of people!" Wesley murmured to himself, as he gazed at the ship towering over him. Bristling with antiaircraft guns, the carrier's control tower rose in tiers like a titanic steel wedding cake hanging on one side of its wide, pancake-flat flight deck.

How could such a top-heavy, lopsided vessel keep itself aright on the sea? Wesley thought back to the boat he crossed the Atlantic in, how its pointed prow rose and fell in those massive waves, slicing the water in geysers of spray. He started to tremble, remembering the trip, remembering how quickly the sea could swallow something as huge as an aircraft carrier.

"You all right, son?" Ed patted Wesley's shoulder.

"Yes, sir." Wesley rubbed his forehead with his scratchy woolen gloves to push the nightmare crossing out of his head. He'd gotten better at controlling his awful flashbacks by concentrating on something around him that was tangible and real.

So he shifted to looking at the crowd. Way down the length of the carrier was a small platform where a lady was supposed to shatter a bottle of champagne on the hull to christen it. Long streamers of American flags dangled from the ship's deck to the platform where sat admirals and captains and dozens of invited guests.

"Where's your daddy?" Wesley asked Freddy.

Freddy leaned over the railing and pointed to a lower dock right on the waterline. "He gets to knock free the under-timbers when the lady cracks the bottle on the hull. Here's how it goes: A lady the navy asked to do the honors will shout"—Freddy adopted a high pitched voice—"'In the name of the United States I christen thee the USS *Ticonderoga*.'" He switched back to his own tenor. "Then she smashes the bottle on the bow to bless it. The ship's supposed to glide magic-like down the shipway ramp into the water, like the lady set it a-sailing with her little tap of a bottle. But it doesn't move until my daddy knocks free those timbers."

Wesley peered at the dozens of men in work jumpers down below, packed together, waiting patiently. "Can you spot him?"

"No," Freddy replied. "But I know he's there."

As he spoke, more spectators crowded onto the docks. A white man smelling of tobacco and whisky knocked into Ed with a surly and sarcastic, "Excuse me." He lingered behind them.

Ed stiffened and kept staring forward. He didn't turn around to acknowledge the man's presence or budge from his spot by the railing. Alma tightened her grip on Wesley's shoulder.

The man moved on, grumbling.

"Pay him no mind, son," Alma whispered. "The Lord makes all sorts, even rapscallions." Wesley wasn't sure, but he thought he heard Freddy mutter a bad word.

Before he could puzzle out what that was about, Alma's face brightened. "Look, boys. They'll be starting now."

Way down the dock, elevated from the crowd on the platform, an admiral stepped up to a podium and began speaking. His words didn't carry all the way down the length of the ship to where Wesley stood. But he could hear the man's voice rise and fall. Then there was a ripple of hats coming off as a chaplain led a prayer. Finally, a small woman in a long fur coat and white orchid corsage stepped up to take a bottle hanging from a ribboned rope.

"Come on, little lady," said Ed. "Crack that thing."

"Amen," murmured Alma.

"It's bad luck if the bottle doesn't break," Freddy explained to Wesley.

The crowd waited, hushed. She pulled the bottle back and in a graceful little gesture tossed it. It bounced off the ship like a badly served tennis ball off a court net.

The crowd gasped.

One of the naval officers caught the swinging bottle and gave it back to her.

"Aw, maaaan. They shoulda let my mama crack that bottle," Freddy muttered. "She'd have whacked it. That bottle not breaking is serious bad luck."

"Shush, child." Alma silenced him.

The young woman tried again. This time she hauled the bottle way back, guided by the officer, and threw her whole body toward the ship as she hurled the champagne.

SMASH! Even where they stood, Wesley could hear the shatter of glass and see a spray of fizz from the exploding champagne.

The crowd cheered, whistles blew, the shipyards' sirens blasted, and the waiting tugboats tooted, as down below Freddy's father and his coworkers set the ship free. The *Ticonderoga* slid into the wide James River, parting the waters with a great wake of waves and hope.

"That was brilliant!" Wesley chirped, revisiting the excitement of the morning. They'd spent the afternoon with Freddy's parents and now waited on Washington Avenue outside the dry dock company's main gate for the bus that would take them home.

"You're darn tootin'!" answered Freddy.

It was just a few minutes before five o'clock. The round-the-clock shifts were changing. Even though he was a native Londoner, Wesley had grown so accustomed to the quiet of the Ratcliff farm, he was a bit overwhelmed by the ocean of workers on the street, surging to the dry dock company's gates or flooding out to catch the packed trolley cars going up and down the avenue.

Nearby a truck backfired. Other drivers laid on their horns. Against his will, Wesley started to tremble again. This time because Newport News's hubbub reminded him of the urgency of London at war.

Abruptly, the five o'clock siren sounded, signaling the end of the work day for some, the beginning of it for others. Most didn't react to the blaring sound. But Wesley flinched and stiffened. Being around big ships all day had brought back a lot of very bad memories. Now the siren's wail sounded like the alarm he'd heard over and over again back home when the Luftwaffe was coming loaded with hellfire.

The truck backfired again. It might as well have been a

firecracker going off at his feet. The popping backfire, the siren's wail, threw Wesley back to London.

He looked nervously to the sky, waiting for the first whistling scream of a bomb falling through the air. He backed away from Freddy, not seeing him, only the rush of hurrying people, and waded into the stream of passersby. He needed to find the nearest shelter, quick!

Somewhere, far away, Wesley heard a voice calling him. Then strong hands reached past the crush of bodies and turned him around. "Where you going, son?" Ed guided Wesley back to the bus stop, just as a mud-splattered bus pulled up.

Shaking, trying to reel himself back into Virginia, Wesley let Ed hold him back while everyone else boarded. He, Ed, Alma, and Freddy were the last to step aboard. Rattled as he was, Wesley didn't pay attention to the fact that they walked all the way down the aisle, past plenty of empty seats, to cram themselves into already crowded benches in the back.

"I think you look a mite discombobulated, honey lamb. Better sit with us," said Alma.

Of course he was going to sit with Freddy, thought Wesley; why wouldn't he?

The bus driver pulled the long lever to close the door and started to pull away from the curb. But a few more passengers rushed it, banging on the glass. He let them in. Wesley recognized the faces of two teenage boys who bounded up the steps. They'd been to the Ratcliffs' Halloween party. Behind them came the rude man who smelled of tobacco and whiskey.

As the bus left Newport News and headed toward Richmond along the country highway paralleling the James, Wesley shed his distressing flashback by watching the passing landscape. When dusk fell and he could no longer see much out the window, he and Freddy discussed the pros and cons of the planes the *Ticonderoga* would carry into battle. They speculated where the carrier might sail first.

Then, knowing Freddy loved jokes, Wesley repeated one the twins had told him. "Knock-knock!"

Freddy grinned. "Who's there?"

"Dwayne."

"Dwayne who?"

"Dwayne the bathtub, I'm dwowning!"

The boys burst out laughing.

"Wait, I got one," Freddy said. "Knock-knock."

"Who's there?"

"Boo."

"Boo who?"

"Don't cry. It's only a joke."

The adults sitting around them chuckled. Even the bad-tempered man up front turned around and grinned at them. But only for a moment. He nudged one of the teenagers, who also looked back. They whispered together.

"Say, kid," the teenager called. "Aren't you one of the Brits staying with the Ratcliffs?"

Wesley smiled. "Yes, I am."

"I thought so." The teen smiled too. He gestured for Wesley to come up front. "Come on up here and join us. You don't need to sit in the back of the bus."

"Oh, thanks very much. That's very kind of you," said Wesley. "But I'm fine right here."

The teen's face clouded. "Really, kid, you should come up here." His tone of voice was no longer so friendly. "You don't belong back there."

Wesley was aware of a sudden tense silence in the bus. Ed and Alma seemed to have frozen. Freddy straightened his glasses. He was looking at Wesley with the strangest expression, like he was waiting for Wesley to prove something.

Freddy pointed to a large sign nailed into the seat in front of them that said WHITES on its front. For the first time Wesley realized that only white people were sitting in front of it. All the Negroes on the bus crowded in behind it. He was sitting in the "colored" section.

Wesley looked back to the teen. "Is there a law that says I can't sit here?"

Instantly, the man took his sincere question as back talk. He stood up, whacking the arms of the boys, who then rose out of their seats as well.

"Ed," Alma breathed, nervously putting her hand on her husband's arm.

Suddenly, the bus swerved and pulled over to the side of the road. The driver turned around and opened the door. "No trouble on my bus, gentlemen. Sit down or get off." He was a big man and his blue uniform strained against the muscles in his arms.

The teenagers plopped down immediately. The man squared himself. "You standing up for coloreds, Mac?" the man snarled.

"I'm standing up for my bus. There will be no trouble on it. Get out or sit down. We've got ten more minutes to the terminal. Your choice."

"You gonna make me?" the man challenged.

The bus driver reached below his seat and pulled out a baseball bat. "I see now that you're drunk, mister. I wouldn't have let you on the bus in the first place if I'd realized that. Now sit down or get off before I blow my top."

Grumbling, the man sat.

The rest of the drive the bus was eerily silent. When he pulled into the station, the driver told the man and the boys to get off first. As he stomped down the stairs, the teen who'd invited Wesley to join him turned around and pointed at Wesley. "I'll be lookin' for you, boy."

"Better hang back a few minutes," the driver cautioned Alma, Ed, Freddy, and Wesley. He waited with them as the teenagers and man disappeared down the street, and only then did the five of them step out onto the roadway. "My son is fighting in Sicily. He just wrote that a squadron of Negro pilots from Tuskegee has been mighty helpful there. Mighty helpful. I hope after the war things are different for you folks."

He turned to Wesley and asked, "You ever seen a snapping turtle, son?"

"No sir."

"Well, a snapping turtle is an ornery thing. Once it snaps and bites onto something it thinks is threatening it, it won't let go. A boy like that, who swallows his daddy's nasty attitudes, that kind of boy latches on hard to trouble. Watch yourself."

The driver tipped his hat at Alma and left.

Chapter Fifteen

A month later Wesley learned exactly what the bus driver had meant by his story of the snapping turtle. He and Ron were walking home from school. Usually Ron ignored him, joking and parading with his buddies. Wesley would lag behind, waiting for Freddy to come up the road from his one-room schoolhouse. But this March afternoon, the sky was an unsullied robin's-egg blue, trees were just starting to green up, and Ron was in a strangely friendly mood.

Of course, there also was a history test the next morning, which probably accounted for Ron's suddenly being all buddy-buddy. He was pumping Wesley for all he was worth on facts about the Industrial Revolution. "What's the difference between Rockefeller and Vanderbilt?" he asked.

"Vanderbilt was railroads and Rockefeller oil," Wesley answered dutifully, as Ron scribbled on the study guide Miss Darling had given the class.

"Wait." Ron stopped. "I thought Carnegie was railroads." He looked at Wesley suspiciously. "You trying to trip me up?"

"Carnegie started in railroads, but he switched to steel," explained Wesley, refraining from saying something sarcastic, having learned now not to "worry a wasps' nest" as Mrs. Ratcliff termed asking for trouble. Besides, now that Wesley had Freddy as a friend, Ron's taunts didn't bother him quite as much. And helping Ron with his homework helped keep the peace around the Ratcliff house.

"Steel?" Ron asked.

Wesley sighed. "Yes. He actually is a Scotsman, you know. He . . ."

"Shut up." Ron abruptly stopped him. Coming toward them were two boys on bicycles. Ron quickly folded up the paper and rammed it into his jacket pocket, as the pair swerved to a halt in a show-off shower of gravel.

"Hey, Ronnie."

It was the boy from the bus! Wesley rammed his cap lower on his head to hide his blond curls. He looked down and started scratching the sandy dirt with his toe.

"Hey, yourself," Ron answered.

"Miss you in class, guy." The boy reached out and smacked Ron's arm in a friendly gesture. "It just ain't the same without you."

"Yeah." Ron sounded irritated, reminded that these boys had moved ahead in school while he had flunked a grade. "Whatcha up to?"

"We're heading to Fort Harrison, to ride the earthworks. If

you really move going uphill, you get a good whoop and holler at the top."

The boy was describing the ruined battlements of a Confederate fort. Wesley had ridden the earthworks himself, rattling his teeth as the bike climbed and fell on the moatlike ridges.

"Yeah, I know that. Think I'm a fathead or something?" Ron's aggressive tone somehow came across as friendly posturing with these boys, who grinned at him. "In fact, I bet I can get my bike to fly across the gap between earthworks."

"Get out of town!"

"Seriously." Ron puffed himself up. "Bet ya a nickel!"

"You're on! You can use my bike," the boy from the bus said.

"Swell!" Ron turned to the rider's companion. "What about you, Roy?"

"A nickel? You do know, Ron, that's five whole cents, right?" He held up his fingers as he counted, "One, two, three, four, five."

Ron's face turned red. "Yeah, I know." Ron raised his hand, his fingers extended. "One, two, three, four, five." With each number he rolled down a finger until he made a fist that he shook threateningly. "Ready to put your money where your mouth is?"

The boy from the bus laughed. "Good old Ronnie." He slapped Ron on the back and elbowed his friend to follow. "Let's go."

The trio started off, without Ron saying a word to Wesley.

"What about your pal?"

Ron looked surprised that Wesley was still standing there. So the rider called to him in friendly fashion, just as he had on the bus: "Hey, kid. Come on. Join us."

Wesley ducked his head and shook it, fearing that as soon as he opened his mouth the boy would recognize him.

"Speak up, runt," Ron snarled. Wesley knew that Ron was furious that he'd been caught walking with Wesley—as if they were friends.

"Thanks, but I need to nip home." Wesley replied in his best American accent. But in his nervousness, he blundered into using an English saying.

"Nip?" Ron's friends laughed. "You got some bootleg whiskey on you, kid?"

Wesley didn't dare look up.

Even so, within seconds, the bus rider was onto him. "Wait a minute," he turned to Ron. "Is that the Brit?"

"Yeah," Ron answered with a sigh. "He's the limey. Let's go."

Wesley heard the rider swing his leg over his bike and lower it to the ground.

"Hold up, Ron. This kid humiliated my dad on the bus from Newport News."

"What?" Ron asked.

"Yeah, he was sitting back in the colored section. When I heard him tell a joke with that accent, I recognized him from your Halloween party. Minding my manners, sweet as molasses, I invited him to join us up front. But he sassed us. He said there weren't no law against him sitting back there."

Wesley gasped. "That's not what I said!" he cried, finally looking up, realizing for the first time that his innocent question about segregation laws sounded like a defiant American wisecrack. He'd gotten into hot water like this so many times since coming to the States, not speaking "American English" or knowing American sayings. "All I meant was..."

"You sassing me again, kid?" In three quick strides the teenager was toe-to-toe with Wesley, looming over him. "There was total hell to pay with my old man that night after we got off the bus." The boy's voice was bitter. "As if what happened was my fault or somethin'. That's the thanks I got for being nice to you."

Instinctively, Wesley looked to Ron for help. But Ron's face was all gnarled up. Just like it'd been on the day the mules had dragged Charles, and Bobby had helped Charles instead of helping Ron.

Still staring down Wesley, the boy from the bus threw a barb at Ron. "You should teach this kid the way things are done here, Ronnie. In the country that's saving his skinny ass and his little island. For Negroes in America it's separate but equal."

"Equal?" It just came out of Wesley's mouth. "Are you kidding?"

It was Ron who shoved Wesley first.

Chapter Sixteen

Later that day, Patsy and Charles were walking home, their shift on the aircraft watchtower over. "Oh, Chuck, that's so funny!" Patsy's laughter lifted to the darkening sky. "Why in the world do they wear wigs of horsehair?"

Charles had been describing British courts and the fact that lawyers were still required to wear white, eighteenth-century-style wigs with tightly upturned curls as they argued cases. "What can I say, Pats. Tradition is very important to us. You should see those poor blokes bolting for air raid shelters clutching those wigs on their heads. I saw one old bald barrister lose his once. A good wind blew it off and a dog grabbed it and ran away, growling and shaking the thing like he'd caught a Thames rat."

"Oh, Chuck, how terrible for the gentleman!" But she was laughing all the same.

"Aw, that ain't nothing." Charles was on a roll now. "You

should see the Buckingham Palace guards. They wear black bearskin hats that are a foot and a half tall. My favorite uncle is a Royal Guardsman. He says it's heavy as hell. Oh, sorry, as heck. But all that fur shields his eyes and helps him keep from reacting to the crowd when he's standing guard. That's a big game in England—trying to make palace guards notice you. Better yet, laugh, by doing junk like this." He stuck his thumbs in his ears and wiggled his fingers while sticking out his tongue.

Patsy giggled. "They'd laugh at that for sure."

"Nope. They're trained to stand stock-still. When Wes and I were young, Uncle Trevor used to pretend to stand post and let us try." Charles snapped to attention. "Go ahead, Pats, see if you can get me to smile." Charles fixed his gaze above her head.

"Oh no, that's silly," said Patsy.

But Charles knew how to get her to play along. He'd seen Bobby goad Patsy into joining her siblings' games over and over again with three simple words: "I dare you," he said.

"Okay, mister, you asked for it." Patsy put down the large notebook and books she was carrying. Standing with her hands on her hips, she considered him a moment. Then she stuck her pointer fingers into her dimpled face and twisted, crossing her eyes.

Charles kept staring ahead.

"Oh my gosh, look at that." She pointed behind him with a gasp. "Really, Chuck, look what's coming!"

Charles ignored her.

She faked a little soft-shoe dance.

Nothing.

Frowning, she stood with her arms crossed, tapping her foot, considering her next move. Charles's jacket was open. With a mischievous smile, she reached out and poked his ribs.

Charles caught his breath.

"Aha!" Patsy started tickling him in earnest, the way she did the twins. "Now I've got you!"

Charles burst out laughing, "No fair! You can't touch the guard!" He grabbed her hands and swung her around playfully. "You cheated!" he cried.

Swinging around like a child's game of ring-around-the-rosy, they tripped and fell into a laughing jumble. Patsy's head landed on Charles's chest and she lay there a moment, trying to catch her breath. She rolled over, face to the sky, gulping air to quiet her laughter.

The Ratcliff brothers tumbled all over one another constantly like this, somehow ending up in laughing heaps. Patsy, too. But this was new to Charles. Startled by the scent of her rose-water perfume, the wisps of her silken hair lying across his face, Charles's heart started pounding. He dared to reach up to stroke her head.

But before his hand touched her, Patsy sat up abruptly and pointed to the sky. "Oh look, Chuck, did you see? A shooting star, I'm sure of it. Make a wish, quick." She clasped her hands and closed her eyes.

Charles sat up slowly as he made his own devout wish. Would he ever have the guts to tell her what it was? he wondered.

As they scrambled to their feet, Charles scooped up her notebook and handed it to her. Without thinking, he said, "You know, after the war, Patsy, you should come to London to see the works in the National Gallery. There are paintings by Leonardo da Vinci, Monet, Rembrandt, van Gogh. You're such a good drawer. All artists should see the masters as inspiration for their own work."

"You know about my drawings?" she asked in surprise. For a moment, they both held an end of her notebook.

Uh-oh. He was caught in his snooping. Charles would have come up with some lame fib, like he'd just happened to see them when her notebook had fallen open or some such rot, but he caught the wistfulness and hope in Patsy's question. It demanded honesty. He gave up trying to play it cool. "Yes, I know about your drawings," he admitted. "Why do you hide them? They're beautiful."

"Really?" she asked.

Charles nodded.

"I dunno." She dragged out the words. "I suppose I feel stupid thinking a farm girl can dream about being an artist. Maybe if we lived in London or somewhere like that it might be different. I read that in New York City some girls who can draw well become commercial artists or work for ad agencies." She looked at Charles's face intently as if to gauge his sincerity. "You really think my sketches are beautiful?"

"Oh yes!" he exclaimed.

Patsy looked up at him with such gratitude for his compliments that Charles was totally entranced. "Absolutely, you should dream about becoming an artist, Patsy. I've seen famous art in London, so I know what I'm talking about. Your drawings are beautiful."

Beaming, Patsy gave him a smile that took his breath away. Mesmerized, his own hopes taking over, Charles felt his face slowly lowering toward that smile, those lips, as he spoke. "Beautiful," he whispered, "like you."

HONK! HONK! HONK!

They jumped apart. Patsy stared at Charles with startled bewilderment before she darted away toward the honking car. Charles felt the loss of her nearness like a kick in the stomach.

It was Dr. Thompson in the two-toned Packard he drove to make house calls. He'd stopped in the middle of the road. "I thought that was you, Patsy," he called into the field. "Hop in, you two. I'll give you a lift. I'm on my way to your house. Your family sent word they needed me to stop by. Sounds like there were some shenanigans this afternoon on the way home from school. Ron's arm might be broken."

Chapter Seventeen

"You should have seen me, Charles. Oh, it was smashing!"

Charles gaped in amazement at his baby brother. Wesley's blond curls were matted with dirt, his face scratched, his lower lip split. His trousers were ripped and his knees scraped and bloody. Yet he bubbled with excitement.

"I hit him!" Wesley crowed. "Pow! Right in the old kisser!" He swung his arms at an imaginary punching bag. "Ouch!" He stopped and rubbed his arm.

"Slow down, Wes." Charles put his hand on Wesley's shoulder. "Tell me what happened."

"I'd like to know exactly what happened too." Mr. Ratcliff stood beside Charles. He'd been watching Dr. Thompson mold sticky plaster of paris on Ron's arm.

"Well." Wesley looked over to Ron before answering. "Well." He looked back to Charles. "Well." He scanned the room and realized everyone was hanging on his words.

Wesley took a deep breath. Before that evening he might have told on Ron, exposing him as a bully. It'd be spot-on payback for all the torment Wesley had endured from him. But now? After this afternoon?

He glanced back to Ron, who eyed him defiantly, waiting for Wesley to speak, along with everyone else. "Well, it's like this," Wesley began. "Ron and I were walking home from school—"

"You were? Together?" Both Bobby and Charles interrupted him, surprised.

Wesley hesitated.

"Yeah, we were," snapped Ron. "Want to make something of it?"

"Shush, son." Mr. Ratcliff silenced him. "You may already be in a heap of trouble as it is. No need to dig your hole deeper."

"Oh no, Mr. Ratcliff, it's not like that at all!" cried Wesley. "Ron saved me."

"He did?" Mr. Ratcliff seemed astonished. So did Bobby and Charles.

"Indeed he did!" Wesley hurried to explain in a torrent of words. "You see, I didn't know that Negroes have to sit in the back of the bus. And that I wasn't supposed to be back there. All I was doing was sitting with Freddy."

"Hold on, Wesley. What in Sam Hill does that have to do with Ron?" asked Mr. Ratcliff.

"Oh, right-o. That's doesn't make sense, does it?" Wesley giggled.

Charles exchanged a quizzical glance with Bobby.

"You see, I ran into a spot of trouble with a man and his

son on the bus. You know, the day Freddy took me to see the launching of the *Ticonderoga*. Oh, that was super, that was. It's so enor—"

"Wesley!" Mr. Ratcliff interrupted. "You've already told us all about the big ship, son. Can we stick to tonight, please?"

"Oh! Sorry. Right. But it is connected, Mr. Ratcliff, really. You see, they'd given me a hard time on the bus for sitting with Freddy in the colored section. But the bus driver stopped them. I think the father had been drinking. Anyway, they weren't very happy about it. And then when we were walking home from school today, that very same boy rode up on his bicycle." Wesley hesitated, not sure if he should say that the boy was a friend of Ron's.

Mr. Ratcliff turned to Ron.

"Tommy," Ron muttered.

"Oh," Mr. Ratcliff said shortly. He frowned. "I know the boy... and his father. Please continue, Wesley."

"Well... he said that I had made trouble for him. I honestly hadn't meant to, Mr. Ratcliff. They just didn't understand what I said."

Mr. Ratcliff couldn't help smiling. "Yes, that can be a bit of a problem. But go on now. Tell me what happened... *today*."

"Well..." Wesley pressed his lips together, hesitating about how much to reveal. Then he knew: he would never tattle and tell the Ratcliffs that Ron had been the first to shove him to the ground. That Ron had stood by as the boy from the bus kicked Wesley in the gut. And just watched as the boy's companion pulled Wesley to his feet and slugged him hard in the mouth.

No, Wesley would only tell the Ratcliffs what Ron did next. The part where Ron saved him.

"The boy's friend was holding my arms back so that the boy from the bus—Tommy—could punch me." Wesley choked on the words, remembering the shock of the pain, the look of hate on the boy's face. "Things were going rather black. I thought I might die! But then Ron . . ." Wesley paused and nodded toward Ron. "Ron pulled them off me. He must have thrown Tommy ten feet.

"Thanks to Ron, the two of them left me alone. But they went after Ron because he'd helped me. I couldn't just stand there, since Ron had saved me. Soooooo . . . I tripped Tommy's friend!" Wesley said proudly. "And, and, and . . . when he got up I hit him. I actually hit him!"

Charles's mouth dropped open. So did Bobby's. So did Patsy's.

"Hold on a second, Wes." Mr. Ratcliff interrupted. "Are you telling me that Ron stopped those boys from beating you up?"

"Yes!" Wesley exclaimed.

"And that *you* got into fisticuffs?"

"I did!" Wesley exclaimed again. "Tell them, Ron."

Ron was gaping at Wesley like everyone else. But as it became clear that Wesley wasn't going to rat on him, he slowly smiled. Wesley smiled back.

Charles looked from Ron to Wesley to Ron again, not quite believing what he was witnessing.

"Yup, he did," Ron finally confirmed, adding a "what-of-it" shrug when he saw that his family was looking at him with such surprise.

"So, that's the story," Wesley ended. "Ron saved me. Then... oh my... I guess it can be said that I..." Wesley stopped and pulled himself up tall. "Yes, I saved him!" He giggled in delight with himself.

Everyone waited for Mr. Ratcliff to speak again. Wesley's story was such the opposite of what they all had expected to hear that it took Mr. Ratcliff a moment to find words. "Normally your mother and I don't approve of fistfights. You know that, boys, right?"

They nodded. Wesley knew Mr. Ratcliff was obliged to say so.

"But, Ronald." He paused. "I have to say I'm mighty proud of you, son."

"Me too, little brother," added Bobby.

"Really?" Ron's face completely changed as it lit up. Like when a shaft of sunshine managed to break through England's thick gray cloud cover, thought Wesley with amazement. Ron's face was suddenly that different.

"Awww, I guess he's sorta kinda part of the family, right?" Ron addressed his question to his father and Bobby, but didn't wait for an answer. "Nobody messes with my family when I'm around. Besides"—he glanced at Wesley and a playful smile spread slowly across his face—"nobody gets to punch the limey except me."

Wesley laughed.

Ron laughed back.

Bobby sat down beside Ron and tousled his hair. The brothers grinned at each other. At that moment, Wesley noticed for the first time how Ron was simply a younger, slightly more rugged image of Bobby, almost handsome even.

"When it dries, I get to sign your cast first," Bobby announced. "I'm gonna write 'Ron to the rescue. Brothers in arms forever.' Ha-ha, right? Get it? In arms?" He elbowed Ron, who flinched in pain. "Sound good, little brother?"

"Yeah." Ron's voice was raspy as he answered. "Sounds great to me, brother."

With so much going on, it wasn't until after dinner that Mrs. Ratcliff remembered she held a letter for Charles. "I'm so sorry, sugar, we've had so much excitement this afternoon, I plumb forgot to give you this." She pulled a transatlantic envelope from her apron pocket.

"Who's it from?" Wesley asked, hoping it was from their parents. Oh, but wouldn't he have grand news for them in his next letter! he thought proudly.

"William," Charles answered as he tore it open and read. His face fell. "Oh, he's cricket captain now."

Wesley knew that if he were home, Charles would probably have that honor.

Then Charles's face turned white. "Wes, the school got a direct hit last month."

"What?"

Charles passed him a newspaper clip from the *London Times*. "They ran a photo. Look, there's William, helping to clean up the mess." He pointed to several boys wading through scattered bricks, beams, and hunks of glass. Charles stood up from the table. He was trembling. He skimmed the letter again. "There's a crater in the cricket pitch, shrapnel all over the rugby field. The library's plaster ceiling collapsed. The entrance gates and their statues are destroyed. Remember those jolly old stone lions?"

Wesley nodded.

"Gone. Obliterated."

"Was anyone . . . Was anyone hurt?"

"No, by some miracle, not seriously. Just some nasty cuts from the glass. The bombs missed the dormitories. No one was in the library that late at night, thank God." Charles dropped his arms and the letter fell to the table. "William's saying it'll take weeks for them to clean up because so many chaps have left, chicken about the Blitz." He looked at his little brother, shame on his face. "I should be there helping."

A knock on the door interrupted.

"Land's sakes, what a day we've had," Mrs. Ratcliff said as she went to the front door. "What on earth could it be now?"

At the kitchen table, the family heard the door pop open and Mrs. Ratcliff's surprised, "Clayton!"

Now Patsy's face turned white. It was their cantankerous neighbor, Clayton Forester, Henry's father. He'd never come over to pay a friendly visit. He barely spoke to anyone. Charles and Bobby exchanged a knowing glance. Mr. Forester would never come over unless there was . . .

"Bad news, I'm afraid, girl." Mr. Forester stood in the kitchen doorway, hat in hand. "Lilly would have come to tell you herself, but she's tore up. I thought you should know, given his being so sweet on you." His gravelly voice broke and he swallowed hard. "We received a telegram. Our boy's missing in action. Henry's plane went down somewhere over France. That's all we know right now."

Mr. Forester put his hat back on and tugged its brim down so his eyes were hidden. Awkwardly, he attempted to reassure Patsy. "Henry's a smart boy. If he made it to the ground alive, he'll figure things out. I just hope I toughened him up enough." With that, he turned abruptly, grunting a "good night," and left. Mr. Ratcliff saw him out the door.

Frozen to her seat, Patsy sat shaking her head. "No," she whispered. "No."

Charles reached for her hand to comfort her. But Patsy jerked it away, shooting him a glance that he could read easily. She'd almost let Charles kiss her while the boy she loved was shot down, maybe captured, maybe on the run, maybe dead in a comet of flames. She'd never let him that close ever again.

Putting that hand to her heart, Patsy rushed out of the room. Her mother followed.

That's it, Charles told himself. Who was he kidding? Patsy would never love him. And it was dishonorable for him to even hope for it. Her beau was off fighting the Nazis, partly to liberate his and Wesley's country from terror. How ungrateful could he be?

More to the point, it felt to Charles as if his school chum's letter had implied that he was a coward for not being in London when the city desperately needed every able hand—a sense of guilt that had dogged Charles ever since he had walked up the gangplank of the ship evacuating him to America.

Wesley finally seemed capable of taking care of himself. There was no longer an overriding big-brother responsibility tying Charles to Virginia. England needed him more.

Charles was going home. He wasn't going to waste any more time negotiating the matter with his father, hoping for permission from overseas. No, Charles would wait until the Ratcliffs had fallen asleep. Then he would find that canoe Wes had told him about, float down the river like he'd been imagining for months, and stow away on a freighter bound for Great Britain.

20 March 1944

Dear Dad,

I am writing this in case something bad happens on the high seas. Tonight, I received a letter from William, telling me about the direct hit on the school and how hard it will be to piece the grounds back together. It made me feel such a coward for not being there to help my mates. So I am coming home, Dad. I cannot wait any longer. I am going to catch a cargo ship leaving from Hampton Roads tonight.

The Ratcliffs could not have been more kind, and it was right to send Wes to safety away from the Blitz. I needed to come along to take care of him. He should stay here in the States for the duration. He's only eleven, after all. But I am fifteen now, Dad, and more grown up than you can imagine since you have not seen me for three and a half years. I wonder sometimes if you would even recognise me.

I know you and Mum want to protect us. But I am ready now to make my own decisions about what I should do, about what I can handle, about what is right. Please tell Mum I love her.

Yours, Charles

Dearest Mummy,

I have had such a WONDERFUL day! I hope you will be proud of me. I am sure Charles is and that Dad would be as well. I got in a FISTFIGHT, just like in the Westerns! I SAVED Ron! Now he and I are going to be FRIENDS like the Lone Ranger and Tonto! I think I finally fit in here–isn't that ~~bully~~ swell?

Your loving son,
Wesley Bishop

Chapter Eighteen

As the back door clicked shut loudly, Charles grimaced. *Don't wake up, dogs, please don't wake up.* A moment passed. Nothing. He turned, tiptoed down the steps, and escaped into the darkness.

It seemed a fine night for running away. The black sky was splashed with thick, billowy clouds, but the moon was almost full and its white light lit up the earth. The Ratcliffs' acres of winter wheat rippled in the cold March wind, and in the moonshine the knee-high blades glittered silver, then sage, then emerald green as they bowed and rose, bowed and rose again.

Charles memorized the sight of them—planting that crop was one thing he'd done right to help the Ratcliffs, he reassured himself, trying to squash the regret rising up in him about running away. He hurried on past the fields. It was already one A.M. He was setting off far later than he'd hoped. Wesley had been so excited about the fight with Ron's buddies and his newfound courage that he'd dashed off a triumphant note home and then babbled to Charles until midnight.

Charles had to wait until his little brother was soundly asleep, his breathing slow and steady, before he dared write a note to his father explaining what he was about to do, especially if the worst happened out there on the ocean. He tacked it up on the wall, on his map marking Allied advances, knowing Wesley would find it there and read it himself. Then he shoved a few things into a pillowcase and crept down to the kitchen.

In a mere four hours, Mr. Ratcliff would be getting up. That was barely enough time for Charles to make his way to the marshy land overlooking Turkey Island, where he hoped to find the canoe Wesley had described. He needed to be well on his way down the river before Mr. Ratcliff could get in his truck and come looking for him.

That was his plan: Locate the canoe. Float it downriver, past Weyanoke Point, past Jamestown, past Hog Island, to the Newport News–Hampton Roads docks. There he'd stow away on a cargo ship, hiding in one of its covered lifeboats on deck. Once the freighter cleared the Chesapeake Bay and was out into the Atlantic, he'd reveal himself to the captain and offer to work in exchange for transport to England. He had a little pocket money. He'd pay the captain to telegraph a message to the Ratcliffs then.

Piece of cake. Hadn't Huck Finn floated a rickety old raft down the Mississippi? Charles knew that between him and Norfolk yawned sixty miles or so of deep water, with strong, changeable tidal currents. But Twain wouldn't write such a story if it couldn't be done, Charles reassured himself.

He turned to say good-bye to the clapboard farmhouse where he'd known a lot of joy, a catch in his throat. Sorry if I scare you, Wes, he thought. Sorry, Bobby, for not telling you beforehand. Although Charles was sure his best friend would understand. Bobby would get the question of his honor being at stake. And Patsy, would she be sorry at all to see Charles gone?

As he stood in such thoughts, a dark shadow raced across the grass toward Charles, and a rush of air *swooshed* over him. *"God's teeth!"* he cried out, ducking.

Whoo-cooks-for-you. Whoo-cooks-for-youuuuuuu.

Charles turned just in time to glimpse the tail end of a barred owl as it swooped into the trees, hooting as if trying to remind him of the people who'd cooked for him, sheltered him, cared about him during his country's troubles. For a moment, he hesitated. But only for a moment. Charles pushed off his guilt by getting mad at himself. *You're that spooked when strafed by an owl, Bishop? How will you hold up against the bloomin' Luftwaffe?*

Charles squared his shoulders and went on his way.

Back at the house, Wesley murmured in his sleep. He flipped over, flipped again, dragging the sheets around his neck. He was choking. He was drowning. He opened his mouth to call for help, but waves gushed in, shoving water down his throat as he clung to an overturned boat. *Charles!*

Charles was clinging to the overturned boat too. It was raining, great black sheets of rain. *Charles!* Wesley lunged for Charles's hand as it seemed to slip down the boat into the water.

Another wave spun the boat around and around, dunking Wesley. He resurfaced. He was all alone.

"Charles!" Wesley shrieked, sitting bolt upright in bed, awash in sweat and terror. He rubbed his forehead and started to search under his pillow for his stuffed koala, but stopped himself. "It's only a dream," he said aloud to steel himself.

Suddenly there was a great crash of wind on the northwest-facing window, and within seconds a hard rain hammered the tin roof.

Wesley had grown up in England's torrential rains, but he still marveled at how suddenly weather changed in the States. He picked up his wind-up clock. Four forty-five A.M. Only fifteen minutes before the alarm would ring. He might as well dash to the bathroom before anyone else got up.

Easing out of bed, Wesley tiptoed toward the doorway so as to not wake Charles. Wesley was glad Charles had slept through his nightmare-shouting this time, especially now that Wesley had proven he could stand up for himself in a fight.

In fact, the dream was weird in that it wasn't so much Wesley in danger as it was Charles. Like Charles needed him, for once. Wesley looked over at his big brother's bed.

It was empty.

Bobwhite. Bob-bob-white.

Just as Wesley had on the day of the Thanksgiving hunt, Charles followed a quail call to a field of tangled wildflowers and grasses, matted now with early morning frost. He waded through it, his pants and shoes getting wet and cold from the ice crystals. The crisp air was laced with far-carrying smells, and he could just barely catch the scent of a large body of moving water. He turned east.

Charles emerged on the James River oxbow, a big, meandering U the river took around Turkey Island. There was the makeshift camp Wesley had described. Charles sighed in relief and leaned over, resting his hands on his knees for a moment. He'd walked for two straight hours, covering six or seven miles. He was already exhausted.

The moon was setting. Looking west over his shoulder, Charles saw a mountain range of dark clouds massing in the distance. Rain's coming, he thought, better hurry.

Passing the ashes of a campfire, tripping on a pile of discarded oyster shells, Charles found his way to the shed Wesley had described. Just beyond it was a forest of marsh grasses, spreading into the dark water. A long silvery streak of moonlight lay across the narrow oxbow like a shimmering bridge to Turkey Island. Charles trotted to the shoreline.

"Okay, Wes, where the blazes is that canoe?" Panicked that the boat might not be where Wesley said, Charles thrashed the marsh grasses as he searched.

Frawnk! Awk-awk-awk. Startled, an enormous great blue heron lifted off in flight, almost smacking him in the face with its six-foot wingspan. Charles fell back on his butt, shouting, "Damn it, Wes!" as if somehow his brother was to blame for his being startled.

But sprawled on the ground Charles could see a dark, solid mass through the swaying veil of grasses. There was the canoe, overturned and pulled up onto the ground. It'd been carefully hidden in a patch of tall, wispy wild rice, probably to prevent someone from doing exactly what he was about to do—steal it. "All's fair in love and war," he muttered, trying to convince himself.

The nine-foot, wood-and-canvas canoe was hard for Charles to flip over by himself. But he was absolutely determined, and somehow managed to yank and tug it to the marsh's edge. As its pointy tip struck water, the canoe suddenly slid along easily, almost like it was helping, like the taste of river woke it up. Charles had to rush to leap in before it floated away without him.

The canoe bobbed and swayed as Charles settled himself on a caned seat in its back end. He'd never been in a canoe before. For a moment he marveled at its graceful construction. Tightly spaced strips of golden wood bent upward in a long slender ribcage. Its skin was a bright green canvas. It looked like a fish, he thought with a smile. It should slice through the water quickly.

It would, of course, with proper paddling. But Charles had no idea how to do that. He'd only been punting along the quiet Cam River in Cambridge. He'd propelled that small, flat-bottomed boat by plunging a pole into the shallows and pushing off the riverbed.

Charles took up the canoe's paddle. Shaped like a long wooden spoon, the paddle was almost as tall as he was, and heavy. But he'd gotten strong playing American football. Charles thrust the blade into the water, pulling it backward hard.

The canoe staggered and spun to the right. Charles tried again, only turning the boat completely around this time, heading back to shore. Cursing, he stuck the paddle into the water to push off the muddy sand bottom. He nearly lost it altogether as the paddle temporarily stuck and the canoe lurched back into the current.

After ten minutes of flailing and splashing, spinning and rocking, Charles figured out he should place just the bottom tip of the paddle into the water. To go forward in a straight line, he needed to alternate on which side of the boat he did his strokes. Only then did he move along with the tide.

"Hot dog!" Charles exclaimed. "Now I've got it!"

The canoe skimmed along peacefully, with Turkey Island close on Charles's right. He paddled steadily, as the first glimmer of dawn skipped along the water, like a stone thrown flat from the horizon. He watched a muskrat swim half-submerged, then scramble out onto a mound of sticks. A hawk threw itself into flight from a snag in a grove of ghostly gray sycamores. A colony of seagulls that had slept through the night on the quiet swells of the oxbow took off in a flurry of white wings and shouting to search for breakfast.

Relishing what he figured would be his last glimpses of Virginia, Charles happily saluted the low-hanging willow oaks that dipped themselves into the shoreline waters. "Cheerio, trees! Wish me luck!"

Then the little canoe rounded the southeast corner of Turkey Island and hit the main channel and rushing currents of the James River.

Chapter Nineteen

Tap, tap, tap. Wesley knocked urgently on the door to the Ratcliff brothers' bedroom.

Ron opened it halfway, suspicious. "Now, listen here. Just because we've called a truce doesn't mean we're best pals all of a sudden. No need to walk to school together, you know." But then he noticed Wesley's clothes were soaking wet. "You okay? What gives?"

"It's Charles. I've looked for him everywhere—the barn, the woodshed, the chicken houses, the root cellar. I can't find him. He didn't sleep in his bed last night. Do you suppose someone's kidnapped him, like the Lindbergh baby? Or like that Robert Louis Stevenson book—the one about David Balfour? You know the one I mean?"

"No," Ron guffawed. "Besides, who'd bother kidnapping Chuck? It's not as if he's some famous person's kid or anybody who's real talented or nothin'. Don't start with all your dumb make-believe games again, Wes."

The fact Ron used his name—for the very first time—instead of "runt" or "limey" startled Wesley and stopped his panic. "Right. You're right."

"Of course I'm right."

For a moment the boys stared at each other, thinking. Suddenly, Wesley knew. "I think Charles has run off," he whispered.

"What? That's nuts!"

From inside the room, Bobby pulled the door open wide. He was buttoning up his flannel shirt. "What's going on, boys?"

Ron answered. "He thinks Chuck's run away."

Bobby frowned. "What are you talking about? He would have told me if..." Bobby trailed off. "He was acting kind of weird last night."

Wesley nodded.

"He did seem mighty upset by that letter," Bobby continued, thinking out loud. "He's forever talking about how he should be helping the fight in England. Do you suppose...?"

Wesley nodded. "I think he's trying to get home."

"Aww, get out of town," said Ron. "What's he going to do, swim?"

Wesley felt a sudden sharp pang in his heart and that terrifying sensation of choking. He gasped. "The canoe!"

"What canoe?"

"The canoe that belongs to—" Wesley stopped himself. "Oh, never mind. I told Charles about a canoe I saw near Turkey

Island Creek when we were hunting at Thanksgiving. I bet he's going to try to take it downriver!"

Another vicious surge of wind and rain pelted the house.

"Good Gawd Almighty," breathed Bobby. "He'll drown for sure in this squall. Come on. Let's go. There's no time to lose!"

On the river, Charles was paddling out of the protective shield of Turkey Island, not realizing that a tempest lurked there, waiting for him.

Its first blast of wind shoved him so hard he nearly went over the side of the canoe. The next gust slapped the canoe itself into a spin. Then, leaping and bucking, the tiny boat was caught up in the strong currents of the James's main channel and rushed downstream, Charles facing backward.

"God's teeth!" he cried.

Charles back-paddled desperately, trying to regain some control of the slender little craft. But in the choppy swells, he merely thrashed at the water. The canoe lurched side to side. Waves splashed up into it in bucketfuls. Within moments, Charles was ankle deep in water.

Another explosion of wind shoved the canoe into a swirling eddy of angry water. The canoe turned around and around. Finally, it squirted out into jarring whitecaps in the middle of the widening river. In horror, Charles realized that he was nearing where the Appomattox and the James rivers converged in a crashing tug-of-war of currents, turbulent even on a mild day. He'd seen it before from the shoreline, the day of the turkey shoot. Bobby had commented then that it was one of the most dangerous spots on the river.

Get back to shore! his mind screamed.

He paddled frantically against the current. *Please, oh, please.*

Charles heard rain pounding in a torrent down the river, coming straight at him like a freight train hurtling along its tracks. He stopped midstroke, as he helplessly watched the downpour overtake him. What could he do? There was an inevitability to what was about to happen—like a torpedo racing toward a ship.

Charles was engulfed.

A black waterfall of rain battered him. He clutched the wet, slippery paddle as best he could. He slammed it into the water. *Pull! Pull!* But a massive surge of waves jerked the paddle out of his hands. The boat tipped, dumping Charles into the freezing water.

He felt himself sinking.

Swim, Charles!

Somewhere in the watery blackness, Charles thought he heard Wesley's voice, crying out as he did during his nightmares, urging a drowning man to fight for his life.

Swim!

Charles fought his way up. He bobbed to the surface, gagging and coughing. The back end of the canoe knocked into him. In a moment, it would be gone, washed away. In a moment, Charles would have nothing to keep him afloat. In a moment, he could die.

Catch it, Charles! Now!

Kicking hard, Charles lunged for the overturned canoe, just like he had for Bobby's football passes. The canoe bucked and dunked him. But Charles held on. He wrapped both his arms around its pinched-flat point, clasping his hands together to build a stronger grip. He pressed his face against the green canvas, his head just barely bobbing above water.

Hang on, Charles! For God's sake, hang on.

Charles made himself think about the six young evacuee boys who survived when their ship, the *City of Benares*, was sunk by Nazi U-boats. Those children had floated on high seas for eight days before being found—surviving on half a biscuit and one sardine a day. If they could do that, he could do this.

Stiff upper lip. Don't be downhearted. His mind recited the commands British officials had given him and Wesley as they climbed the gangplank to sail to America.

Surely the storm will push the canoe toward shore, he told himself. Eventually.

Stiff upper lip. Don't be downhearted. Charles repeated the British mantra over and over in a bizarre singsong of confusion and determination.

But after a while, trembling in the frigid waters, spluttering against the brutally constant waves, all Charles could do was concentrate on the feel of his clasped hands. Concentrate on keeping his fingers locked together. Concentrate on spitting out water and breathing in air.

All else was blackness, water, and cold.

"This is it!" Wesley ran into the Chickahominy hunter's camp, Bobby following.

"Hey, Bobby," Ron shouted, thigh deep in wild rice grasses. "Someone's dragged something into the water from here."

Bobby came to look at the trail of flattened grasses and scratched mudflats. "Good scouting, Ronnie!" He clapped his brother's shoulder. Then he looked across the waters. Now even the oxbow, usually quiet and serene, was all churned up by the wind and rain. "This is bad."

Wesley looked up at Bobby with mournful eyes. "Are we too late?"

He could see Bobby clench his teeth. And when he spoke, Bobby didn't answer Wesley's question. "Come on. Let's get back to the truck."

The three of them raced through the rain, through the field, through the woods, to the truck, parked by the roadside. Bobby had only been driving for a few weeks, and the trip around Curles Neck had been wild, worsened by the fact the truck's headlights were still painted over with only a narrow slit for the beams to shine through—a required blackout precaution. In the pelting rain, Bobby could barely see. But none of them complained, or thought about the deep trouble they faced for having taken the truck without asking Mr. Ratcliff.

"Where do we go now?" was all Ron asked.

"Down toward Shirley Plantation," Bobby answered. "Here's

my thinking. Charles has got to get all the way down the oxbow before he reaches the main channel. If we hurry and get to the point of Eppes Island, we may be able to see him coming downriver."

Ron and Wesley clutched the dashboard, as Bobby swerved around a corner. "What'll we do then?"

"We'll figure it out when we get there," muttered Bobby, as he jerked the big steering wheel to dodge a thick branch that had fallen into the road.

They drove for ten minutes in tense silence, punctuated only with cries of "Look out!" when Bobby encountered ponds of standing water from the downpour. Finally, they came to a grinding stop, sliding on wet gravel on the border of Shirley Plantation. The beautiful old house was the first of many English plantations established along the James, in operation since the mid-1600s. It'd been built there for good reason—the site commanded a clear view up and down the river, right where it suddenly widened and flexed its currents before joining with the Appomattox River.

The boys scrambled to the edge of a bluff. Holding hands to their foreheads to shield their eyes against the blasting wind and rain, they squinted and peered west up the waters toward Turkey Island. They spotted floating logs and debris rushing along the waves, thrown into the water by the storm. But no canoe.

They turned left toward the east, looking to where the James suddenly bloated to one mile across. Nothing but bullying waves in a wide, angry flood of water.

Wesley dropped his hand and hung down his head in misery. He knew too well how quickly stormy water could suck someone under, never to resurface. *Where are you, Charles? Please show me where you are.*

Suddenly, Wesley cried out. He tugged on Bobby's sleeve and pointed. Down by the rocks was a crumpled canoe. Lying beside it, facedown, was Charles.

27 May 1944

Dear Dad,

I know Mr Ratcliff telegrammed about my pneumonia and nearly drowning in the James River. You must be angry with me for running away and showing such ingratitude to the Ratcliffs. Believe me, I kick myself for it every day. When the doctor realised my lungs were closing up, he treated me with a new medicine called penicillin. It is made from mould, of all things, and is frightfully expensive. The dose cost Mr Ratcliff $20! (He could have bought 250 loaves of bread for the family with that money.) But he did not hesitate to pay for it. I felt like such a heel.

So, I am working as the soda jerk at Mr Epstein's store after school. I had to give up playing baseball, which I should have been good at, since it is very like cricket. But I owe the Ratcliffs that $20. I make ice cream sundaes and am paid $1.50 for each afternoon. I give half of it to Mrs Ratcliff.

When school ends next week, I shall work the farm doubly hard, too. Mr Ratcliff has forewarned us that when we harvest the winter wheat and plant corn, he has to hire German POWs. He wants to clear fifteen new acres to plant tobacco, too. Breaking ground for new fields will take a lot of labour. I will try to behave while they are here.

The POWs are hard for me to tolerate, though, Dad. The guards bring them into the drugstore sometimes for a Coca-Cola after working a farm. Some act like 'der Führer' will arrive in the States any day—as if we Allies are not on the brink of taking Rome and invading France. Last month, they refused to work on Hitler's birthday, and paraded around their POW camps, singing, to celebrate it!

But back to my confession. You may notice I said I give half my pay to Mrs Ratcliff. When I ran away, I took a man's canoe. It got pretty mangled. He is a Chickahominy named Mr Johns. He actually built the canoe himself. I have helped him repair it. (Wesley did too. He is quite bats about being with a real Indian.) But Mr Ratcliff says I still owe Mr Johns the price of a new canoe—$37. And he is quite right. So I give the other half of my pay to him.

Wesley and the brothers are totally wizard about my running off and causing such trouble. They think it rather a daring lark on my part. When I was sick, Mrs Ratcliff called me, 'Poor little thing,' which was humiliating, but I am glad she is not mad. Mr Ratcliff, however, remains stern with me, which is proper. Patsy hardly speaks to me. But she rarely talks with anyone, really, for long. She is all torn up about her beau, Henry, being MIA.

It is a bad business. I promise to make you proud of me again someday.

Your son,
Charles

Dearest Mumsy,

I do hope you GET this letter. The Richmond newspapers keep warning that mail to England may be held up as a security measure because of the coming invasion. The Yanks have already stopped letters from you. They are worried some silly Brit might spill the beans about the place and day since the Allied armies are gathered in England. They do not know what a tight-lipped lot we are, do they?

Besides, everyone assumes our troops will cross where the English Channel is narrowest and land at Calais. It is just a matter of when. Mr Ratcliff says the date will be decided in part by the moon, the tides, and the weather, since they can all make waves along the French coastline too rough. The army is warning there will be a lot of casualties, but that the enemy better watch out! The Yanks are so confident about things. Ron says the D in D-day stands for 'Doomsday for Dopes!' Ha-ha!

That reminds me! Not to brag, but I do hope you two are proud of me for finding Charles when a storm nearly DROWNED him. Bobby and Ron and I went after him in the truck in a dreadful rain. It was bucketing down. We nearly DIED on the road!

I had told Charles about a canoe I had seen. So we went there first, but he had already set off. So we had to figure out where the river might carry the canoe. Then we drove there as fast as a Spitfire! It was like solving a MYSTERY. We were just like the Hardy Boys piecing together clues and braving danger!

Since then I have helped Charles and Mr Johns rebuild his canoe. Mr Johns is a Chickahominy Indian. It surprised me that his name is so American-sounding. I thought it would be Powhatan or Sitting Bull or something like that. He has taught Charles and me a lot about the rivers and forests around here and the ways of native people, as Mr Johns calls them.

Now I am ready for another adventure! Ron and I are planning one, actually. Freddy told us about a secret...
OH! I suppose I should not say. I shall just close the way the Lone Ranger show does–'Tune in next week for another exciting episode!'

Your loving son,
Wesley Bishop

Chapter Twenty

"Whoa, mules." Charles hauled back on the reins. Belle and Jake stopped, swishing their tails against flies that instantly landed on them. Charles pulled off his straw hat to mop his forehead with a handkerchief. "How can it be this blasted hot already on June sixth?" he mumbled, rubbing his eye against a gnat that had flown in. He knew another summer scorcher and drought could ruin the Ratcliffs. Charles frowned, thinking of the extra burden he'd put on them financially.

He glanced over at Mr. Ratcliff and six German POWs struggling to dig up the stumps of trees they'd cut down the day before so Charles could then plow up the earth for tobacco seed. He couldn't believe Mr. Ratcliff had to pay the army $3.50 a day in wages for each of them. Charles fumed, knowing the POWs pocketed eighty cents of that fee themselves to use in their camp canteen, buying beer or milk and cigarettes. He seriously doubted Allied airmen being held in Nazi stalags were afforded such niceties.

Irrationally, Charles glared at the lone U.S. soldier guarding the detail. He was sitting in the shade, cradling his rifle and reading a newspaper. *How can the Yanks be this lax? Don't they know what Nazis are capable of?*

But they don't, do they? Charles reminded himself irritably, bitterness rising up inside of him. *Their homes and schools hadn't been destroyed. Wait until more of their sons and friends and fathers and brothers and cousins die in battle. Then they might.*

Charles rammed his hat back on his head and flapped his hand against the cloud of gnats swarming him. A POW straightened up to do the same thing, and Charles noted with a perverse sense of satisfaction that the prisoner's blue cotton shirt—where PW was stenciled in big white letters—was sticking to his back. The man was drenched in sweat. All the Germans were. The Tidewater humidity was a brutal adjustment for anyone not born in the area.

Of course, several of the POWs had served in North Africa, part of Rommel's elite panzer divisions, and should be used to heat by now, Charles thought. He easily identified them by their rough manner, their discipline. They were tall, muscular, blond, haughty—perfect Aryan specimens. They probably had the telltale "SS" tattoo under their armpits, marking them as true believers, devotees of Hitler's racist beliefs. The tattoo that told Nazi medics to attend to them first when faced with a lot of German casualties.

The other two POWs were younger, slight of build, more wary, quiet. One had a pretty choirboy face and looked like he didn't even shave yet. He couldn't have been that much older than Bobby, speculated Charles. His name was Günter. He spoke excellent English in proper British accent and with old-world politeness when he translated Mr. Ratcliff's instructions to his fellow prisoners.

When Mr. Ratcliff had asked how he spoke English so well, Günter explained with noticeable pride that his father had been a philosophy professor and a great lover of English literature. Then he lowered his voice a bit as if his father could overhear him. "But I prefer your American writers. Like the poet Walt Whitman. Oh, and Fitzgerald. His *Great Gatsby* is magnificent. As well, I love Scott Joplin's ragtime music. Do you have piano? I will play you some!" He'd been very disappointed when Mr. Ratcliff said they did not.

"How in the world did you end up in the Nazi army, son?" Mr. Ratcliff asked, clearly pitying a rather poetic boy going to war.

"I was to start divinity school when I was drafted as a *Flakhelfer*." Günter glanced at Charles as he spoke. His voice grew careful. "All teens were drafted thus. I manned searchlights. Later antiaircraft guns. But I surrendered in January when *der Führer*'s Bernhardt Line collapsed in Italy. When the Allied army came inland from Anzio."

"Deserteur," one of the burly Germans had hissed, overhearing Günter use the English word "surrender."

Günter's fair face had paled even more. *"Nein! Ich bin es nicht!"* He turned to Mr. Ratcliff. "We were in a forward group. The troops behind us retreated. We were left all alone. We had no choice."

All Charles could think of was that manning ack-ack guns for Hitler meant Günter had served in the ground units of the Luftwaffe—the Nazi air force that had rained death on London. Günter would have trained those cannon on the RAF, maybe on some of Charles's older English chums now flying bombing raids. He might have even been the gunner to bring down Henry, Patsy's missing-in-action beau. It had taken all the self-control Charles had not to attack the boy as Mr. Ratcliff and the German youth chatted.

Remembering the conversation, Charles felt hatred and anger well up in his throat like vomit. He swallowed hard and turned back to his job of plowing. The faster and harder he worked, the fewer hours Mr. Ratcliff would need these cursed POWs, he reasoned with himself.

"Walk on," he shouted, snapping the reins. The mules pulled forward. Charles focused his energy on guiding the plow, relishing how the blade sliced up the ground.

Honk-honk! Honk-honk!

All of a sudden, Bobby drove the truck pell-mell into the field, beeping and swerving, nearly hitting three POWs as they pried up a stump. They jumped back, shovels in hand, cursing, *"Arschloch!" "Dummkopf!"*

"What in Sam Hill are you doing, Robert?" his father bellowed. Then he realized all his sons were crammed in the truck along with Wesley, Ed, and Freddy. They'd been working together on the other side of the farm threshing the wheat fields. "What's wrong?" he asked worriedly. "Is someone hurt?"

Bobby was grinning wildly. "It's happening! Listen!" He threw open the truck door and cranked up the radio.

Crackling and popping, the voice of a radio announcer crowed: "Yes, this is it—D-day, sure to be one of the most important in the history of mankind!"

"Sweet Lord a' mercy," Mr. Ratcliff murmured, dropping his pickax.

In an instant, the truck became a magnet, as its radio announced the advent of the day the world had been awaiting, dreading. Charles knew he'd never forget the sight of Americans, Brits, and Germans alike drawing close to listen, hushed, to what was known of the all-out invasion that would either end Hitler's murderous reign or cement it.

As the radio blared the momentous news about legions of Allied planes, ships, and troops clogging the channel off France, of shelling and bombing, of small landing craft spewing out thousands of soldiers onto the barbed-wire beaches, Wesley climbed out of the flatbed to stand by Charles. They nodded at one another. *Finally.* The invasion had to mean that after four terrible years, Hitler would turn his merciless attention away from Britain to defend his occupation of France, the back door to Germany.

"Yes, the invasion is on!" the announcer fairly shouted, as if to reassure Wesley and Charles it was true. "We first learned of the invasion from scattered reports on German radio. Now General Eisenhower has confirmed that our Allied assault on Nazi entrenchments, the bombardment of what Hitler calls his Fortress Europe, is under way."

Hearing the name Hitler, the POWs inched closer to Günter. One elbowed him roughly. In whispers, Günter began translating the radio's report. As he did, the Germans' faces darkened with scowls.

"Here is what we do know," said the announcer. "Thousands of American and British boys have landed at beaches along a seventy-five mile section of the Normandy coast, from the port of LeHavre, at the mouth of the Seine River, to Cherbourg."

Wesley and Charles—sons of the geography teacher—both gasped. "That's nuts!" said Charles. "That coastline is full of cliffs. The Jerries are sure to have fortified those hills. They'll have such an advantage. They can shoot down on our boys with machine guns as they try to get out of the boats. And the channel is so wide and rough there. Why didn't they go the short distance to the easy beaches of Calais?"

"I bet because that's what Hitler expected, Chuck," Bobby answered quietly. His grin was gone. He looked at Mr. Ratcliff. "Do you suppose Cousin Frank and Cousin Ethan are there?"

His father nodded. "They're in the Twenty-Ninth Infantry Division along with a lot of Virginia boys. There's been plenty of talk at church about their being in the D-day forces." Mr.

Ratcliff turned to Ed. "Isn't your youngest a cook on a battleship somewhere in the Atlantic, Ed?"

"Yes," Ed answered. "We haven't heard from him for a while now. Alma's been worried sick he'd be in this fight."

"Doesn't Mr. Johns have a son in the army too?" Wesley whispered to Charles.

"Yes, he is in a unit of Indians—the Forty-Fifth Division, I think."

"Shhhhh." Ron shushed them.

"It is difficult to know how the battle goes," the announcer explained, "as the fighting is desperate and continues under a barrage of shelling from our bombers flying overhead and from our battleships offshore. But news reporters with the troops tell us that our brave boys are withstanding the German counterfire and that the Nazi strongholds are crumbling."

At this, Günter stopped translating abruptly. He glanced nervously at the other POWs.

The broadcast continued: "The Germans, of course, are claiming that victory will be theirs, that they have captured many American prisoners. But they also admit glider attacks inland and that as many as four divisions of airborne soldiers may have parachuted into France well beyond Normandy fortifications."

Charles thought he saw the smallest of smiles on Günter's face. What did his expression mean? Charles wondered. Was it smug disbelief? Did he think the American radio announcer was making it up? He clenched his hands and rammed them into his overalls' bib pocket to keep them off the young German's throat.

Over the radio came the sound of rustling paper, as the announcer was handed new script. His voice quickened with excitement as he read: "From the BBC, Prime Minister Churchill is sharing new, specific information."

At the mention of Churchill, Wesley and Charles stood a bit straighter. The burlier POWs looked like they might spit on the ground.

"According to Churchill, the Allied invasion forces bristle with more than four thousand fighting ships." The announcer couldn't help exclaiming, "Four thousand! That's miles of ships! Plus eleven thousand airplanes. That's an Armageddon-strong invasion force."

Günter paused once again. His face turned pink, then very white.

Go ahead, kraut, Charles thought. Translate that!

Haltingly, Günter explained to his countrymen the number of Allied ships and airplanes attacking the Normandy beaches. *"Viertausend Schiffe. Elftausend Flugzeuge."*

The largest of them shoved Günter. *"Lügner!"* he yelled. *"Der Führer würde das nicht zulassen!"*

"Nein," Günter cried. *"Ich lüge nicht!"*

"Hey, blockheads!" The U.S. guard finally stood up and shouldered his gun. "Knock it off! Shut up and listen."

There was no need for Günter to translate that.

From the car radio, the voice quoted American soldiers, telling how black and silent the night was as their ships raced across the channel, how it all changed instantly to a world of manmade lightning and thunder that blinded and deafened and killed. "One boy, carrying dynamite, set his jaw as his barge surged toward a beach writhing with soldiers and lit up by explosions, and said, 'They can't stop us!'"

In conclusion, the announcer recounted how Americans had been able to mount the D-day invasion within two and a half years. How the U.S. military had grown from a mere seventeen battleships in 1941, half of those temporarily lost at Pearl Harbor, to more than nine hundred warships. From twelve thousand air force planes to one hundred seventy-five thousand. From an army of three hundred thousand to a fighting force of ten million men and women. All that, he said, from a peace-loving population geared to manufacturing baby buggies and tractors.

Then the radio broadcast shifted to prayers for the safety of Americans fighting in the D-day battle. As the minister began, "Our Father, who art in heaven . . ." Günter lowered his head and clasped his hands dutifully. He didn't notice his fellow POWs glare at him for praying along with Americans. But Charles did.

The hulking POW kicked Günter's ankle and hissed, *"Hör auf zu beten!"*

With a little gasp of pain, Günter unclasped his hands and lifted his head.

Charles looked to see if the American guard had seen the exchange. The guard just laughed. "Radio got your goat, Mac?" He jeered at the bullying POW.

"Was?" the German asked angrily, tightening his grip on the shovel he still held.

"Vhat? Vhat?" The guard mocked the POW as he pulled the bolt of his rifle back and then down, making it clear he would readily shoot the prisoner if he caused trouble.

"Listen!" Bobby interrupted sharply. He lowered the radio's volume and cocked his head. From all directions—from Richmond, Petersburg, Williamsburg—came the faint but distinct sound of church bells ringing, calling.

Everyone froze.

"That's enough for today, boys," said Mr. Ratcliff quietly. "The bells are calling us. I'm sure preachers across the county have thrown open their doors. We have boys to pray for. Let's go to church."

That evening, President Roosevelt addressed the nation over the radio, his voice somber. Already, thousands of American casualties lay along the Normandy beaches. It was only the beginning. He didn't brag about U.S. might, or promise quick or easy victory. Instead, he asked Americans to brace themselves. He reminded Charles of Churchill in the dark days of the Blitz.

"In this poignant hour," said FDR, "I ask you to join with me in prayer. Our sons, pride of our nation, this day have set upon a mighty endeavor . . . to set free a suffering humanity. . . . Give strength to their arms, stoutness to their hearts. . . . Their road will be long and hard. For the enemy is strong. . . . Men's souls will be shaken with the violences of war. For these men are lately drawn from the ways of peace. They fight not for the lust of conquest. . . . They fight to liberate. They fight to let justice arise, and tolerance and goodwill .... For us at home ... give us strength ... in our daily tasks, to redouble the contributions we make.... And let our hearts be stout, to wait out the long travail, to bear sorrows that may come...."

"Amen," murmured Charles, Wesley, and the Ratcliffs, along with millions of other Americans that night.

Chapter Twenty-one

A few days later, Freddy put his pencil on a map and traced a line northward along the crinkly paper. "Just up Willis Church Road a mite, over White Oak Swamp, across the railroad tracks, to Portugee Road."

"How long do you suppose it'd take us?" Wesley whispered. He and Freddy were lying belly to the ground under a persimmon tree, some distance from everyone else. But he still felt the need to keep his voice down for secrecy. The POWs were back on the Ratcliff farm, now helping to plant the cornfields. It was a sweltering day—already 103 degrees at noon. Mr. Ratcliff had shooed them all into the shade for a lunch break. Everyone lay in grumbling clumps, fanning themselves.

"On bikes? About an hour," Freddy reckoned. "Maybe less."

Wesley nodded.

"But Daddy has my bike down in Newport News."

"That's all right," Wesley answered. Now that he and Ron

had become brothers-in-arms, he'd already talked to Ron about being part of this adventure. Every detective needed a strongman. "Ron can carry you on the handlebars of his bike. He's done it plenty with the twins."

"He won't carry a Negro boy on his bicycle."

Wesley thought on that a moment. "He will. He's a better guy than you think. He just needs a little encouragement to know what's right."

Freddy made a face.

"No, really. I think he just needs to feel he's needed somehow. Ron's rather proud of how strong he is. He really wants to know what mysterious secret project the army is working on up there at Elko. He really likes to think you Yanks come up with all the best ideas. I'll remind him that you're the only one who knows the way."

"I'm telling you pure and simple it's some kind of airfield," said Freddy. "I saw something with wings under that netting."

"But why would they have more planes so close to the Richmond Air Base?" puzzled Wesley. "Oh, oh, oh!" He could hardly contain his excitement with the new suspicion he had. "Maybe they've designed some new kind of aircraft. The newspapers have reported our airmen seeing new Nazi planes with strange looking engines and no propellers. Maybe we Allies are developing a rocket ship like Flash Gordon's!"

"Well, whatever it is, they sure don't guard it much," said Freddy. "I swear I could have waltzed right in and made off with one of them planes, easy."

"Maybe we need to let the authorities know that," murmured

Wesley. It was like the guard watching over the POWs. He hardly paid any attention. Charles complained the Germans could wander off and escape if he didn't keep a sharp eye out. Wesley rolled over to check on the camp guard, who'd been propped up against a tree trunk, snoozing and snoring, not even pretending to do his job.

As Wesley turned, he startled in surprise. A few feet from him were the boots and blue jeans of a POW!

Wesley scrambled to sit up, shoving the map to one side, his heart pounding. What an idiot he was! What if the Jerry had overheard about Elko?

It was Günter. "I beg your pardon. I did not mean to frighten you."

Günter watched Freddy hurriedly fold up the map. Was the POW waiting to speak out of politeness? Wesley wondered. Or had he heard everything and so was trying to spot the location they'd been discussing?

When Günter did finally speak, it was haltingly and with embarrassment. "I do not know whom to ask," he began. He held up a large paper sack that contained the lunch Mrs. Ratcliff had made for the POWs. "They will not eat."

"What?" Wesley didn't quite understand what the young German was getting at.

Günter blushed. "They do not like American peanut butter."

Wesley gaped. What a lot of nerve! He'd heard Nazi POWs refused to eat corn, too, saying back in Germany corn was only fed to hogs. Wesley had to admit some American food—like grits—had seemed quite odd to him at first. But he would never have out-and-out refused any of it, even as an invited guest. And these chaps were prisoners!

Günter hurried to add, "I think the peanut butter brilliant."

"Where did you learn to say that?" Wesley asked, irritated to hear a German POW use a favorite British adjective for something being good.

"My father studied at Cambridge."

"Really?"

Günter lowered his voice. "He quite liked his time in England. We are not Nazis. My family never joined the party. In Hitler's Germany, one fights for the Reich or is executed."

He plopped himself down beside Wesley and quieted his voice even more. "Actually, I am relieved your D-day has come. I hope the war ends now. Hitler is destroying the Fatherland. The other prisoners"—he tipped his head toward the beefier Germans—"were in North Africa. They have not seen the destruction of our cities by your air forces. They only witnessed the parades, the speeches, the excitement Hitler made before they left Germany to conquer Africa. They have not seen mothers die in fires"—his voice cracked—"or children crushed in rubble." Günter stopped and looked away.

Were those tears in the Jerry's eyes? Wesley was amazed. He had to blink away the image Günter painted, knowing well the type of horrifying scene he described. Wesley had never thought much before about German families suffering the same kind of terror he and Charles had.

Well, they started it, Wesley thought. If Hitler hadn't decided to gobble up Europe, no Allied planes would be flying over Germany dropping bombs. He squirmed and shifted to sit cross-legged.

His movement pulled Günter's attention back to Wesley and seemed to spark an idea. Günter shifted to sitting cross-legged too, as a child might follow the lead of another to make friends. Günter pulled a book out of his pocket. On its worn, faded cover was an illustration of an American Apache in fringed buckskin, holding a long rifle.

"Do you know the books of Karl May?" he asked. "I grew up reading about the American Wild West through the stories of Old Shatterhand. He is a German engineer who helps build the transcontinental railroad. He befriends an Apache prince named Winnetou. At first they are enemies. Then they become comrades. May wrote many books about their adventures. Together, they fight injustice and corruption. They are my favorite stories since I was your age."

Wesley couldn't help himself. He reached for the book. Günter handed it to him, smiling.

"Blimey!" Wesley tipped the book so Freddy could see the picture of Winnetou as well. "Looks like Tonto, doesn't he?"

"I had hoped to be sent to a POW camp in the west, perhaps Nebraska," said Günter wistfully. "Then I might see a real Indian."

Freddy laughed out loud. "Dang, Wes. This boy sounds just like you!"

Wesley grinned.

Günter brightened and grinned back.

"Actually, there are Indians in Virginia." Wesley pointed

east. "Just down the river was the Powhatan Confederacy. You know, Pocahontas? And there is a Chickahominy native living right now on..."

"What's going on here?" Charles interrupted as he and Bobby hurried up behind Günter. "What the deuce are you doing getting friendly with this Jerry, Wes?"

Wesley's smile vanished. "The POWs won't eat the sandwiches Mrs. Ratcliff made," he defended himself.

Bobby flared up first, saying to Günter, "You insulting my mama's cooking?"

"Oh no! Not I!" Günter protested. "I ate my sandwich. With gratitude." He stood up and nodded respectfully to Bobby. "I beg your pardon for my countrymen's..." He hesitated, his expression hardening. "My countrymen's..." Again he searched for the English word he wanted. "*Hochmut*... mmmm... feeling of importance."

"I suggest you tell them to take what they get, mate," Charles said coldly.

Günter's face flushed with embarrassment. "I did. I told them they were lucky to be given such food. As we cross the ocean, in the prisoner ship, I expected to be beaten and starved. I thought Americans would put us into slave labor when we arrived in the States like... like *der Fürher* did to the Poles and..." He trailed off.

He tried to smile as he continued, but his lips quivered with nervousness. "Instead, the Americans have been very good to us, I tell them. They give us soap and clean clothes and magazines to read, I say. In American POW camp we play football and chess.

Some men paint pictures. Some learn English. I tell them, we should accept American food with thanks."

He looked over his shoulder to where his fellow POWs sat, watching him, scowling. "But they say I better watch out for saying such things. There is punishment for disloyal Germans in camp." He quieted his voice to a whisper: "The *Lager-Gestapo*, the Holy Ghost they call themselves. They drag soldiers they think are not true to *der Führer* into the latrine and beat them. Just like the SS at home. They hurt one of my friends because he likes American jazz. You know, Benny Goodman, Glenn Miller, Tommy Dorsey." Günter imitated playing a clarinet and a trombone as he said the legendary names. But then he grew very serious. "They think I spread American propaganda when I translate Richmond newspapers and radio broadcasts, telling of Allied plans and advancements. They have left chicken bones in my bunk to warn me of..."

Now Mr. Ratcliff walked up and interrupted. "There a peace conference going on here, boys?" he joked.

"Just about the opposite, Dad," Bobby blurted out. "The jerks are saying our peanut butter isn't good enough for them."

Günter looked down sheepishly, as Mr. Ratcliff crossed his arms and squared his feet. Wesley and Charles recognized that stance—he was mad, but trying to be patient, waiting to hear an acceptable reason for bad behavior. "Care to explain that, son?" Mr. Ratcliff asked brusquely.

"I apologize for my rudeness." Günter took a deep breath before continuing. "They do not like peanut butter. They ask for bologna or cheese."

The boys waited for Mr. Ratcliff to speak. Charles bit his lip, wondering how long it'd been since his parents had had a decent bologna sandwich in bomb-riddled England.

"They can eat the peanut butter sandwiches or not eat them," Mr. Ratcliff answered, his voice steely as he contained his anger. "But that's all they will be given. Peanut butter is good enough for me. Good enough for my sons. It is good enough for soldiers who have made war against my country." He put his hand on Günter's shoulder, the way he always did when emphasizing a point with his own sons and the Bishop boys, usually one that required their facing up to doing the right thing, even if it was hard or intimidating. "You tell them that. Exactly as I said. Word for word. Understand me, son?"

His forehead crinkled with worry, Günter nodded.

"No sweetening what I said. I know enough pidgin German to know you soften what the guard says as you translate. I want them to get this message straight up."

"*Jawohl.* I understand."

"Take the bag back to them, then." He patted Günter's shoulder.

Wesley handed Günter his book. Silently, Günter pocketed it. He turned and marched himself back, like he'd just received a sentence to be whipped.

His fellow POWs stood up as he approached. Slowly he recited Mr. Ratcliff's words, "*Der Herr sagt: Sie können die Erdnussbutter Sandwiches essen oder nicht essen. Aber das ist alles, was Sie bekommen werden. Es ist gut genug für die Soldaten, die den Krieg gegen mein Land gemacht haben.*"

The other young, quiet POW took the bag and pulled out a sandwich, dutifully sitting and eating. The others defiantly rammed their hands into their pockets. The man who'd kicked Günter for praying along with the American radio on D-day, stepped toe-to-toe with Günter, looming over him. His voice was too low for Wesley or Charles to hear his words. But the threat in them was obvious.

"That boy isn't going to last among these dyed-in-the-wool Nazis," worried Mr. Ratcliff. "I'm going to tell the guard to keep an eye out for Günter. You boys do, too, when he's here on my farm. There'll be no monkey business on my watch. You hear?"

"Yes sir," Bobby answered.

But as Mr. Ratcliff strode away, Charles couldn't help muttering, "Why should I care if one Nazi bumps off another? If I had my way, I'd take them all out and drop some bombs on them, just like they did to me."

Chapter Twenty-two

The rest of the afternoon everyone worked the fields in a tense silence, speaking only when necessary. They finished plowing the earth into furrows, two feet apart, and fertilized them with manure. Through Günter, Mr. Ratcliff instructed the POWs to make eighteen-inch round mounds of dirt, into which they tucked four corn seeds. It was painstaking work, even with that many men.

Prodded by Mr. Ratcliff, the American guard now paced among the POWs, watchful. Wesley noticed, though, that when the Nazi bully discovered a stone in the dirt, he would dig it out and chuck it at Günter when the American soldier's back was turned.

Ron, Wesley, and Freddy were in charge of filling buckets with water from a vat beside the fields and ladling a bit of it onto each freshly seeded mound. As Wesley passed the POWs, he heard their stomachs rumble hungrily. But they didn't open the bag of sandwiches.

The only people who seemed unaware of the friction and fragile truce among all the workers were the twins. Their chore was to carry tin cups of well water to the thirsty men. But mostly the two boys darted along the fields' edges, laughing and chasing little cabbage white butterflies.

Wesley straightened up and fanned himself with his hat, watching Jamie and Johnny tumble over each other. How could they play like that in this heat? he wondered. All he wanted to do was crawl into the shade and sleep. Standing there, sweating, Wesley was the first to hear a distant spluttering of an engine. He turned toward the river.

A single-engine plane was weaving and staggering through the clouds. Another pilot trainee trying to figure out how to fly, thought Wesley. They'd seen dozens of clumsy flights like this come up the James and turn right across Curles Neck and the Ratcliff farm, as new pilots took off from the Richmond Air Base and then circled back to land on the same runways. Wesley put his hat back on and returned to ladling.

Günter stood near him. *"Das Flugzeug ist in Schwierigkeiten,"* he murmured.

"What?"

He repeated in English. "The plane is in trouble."

"Oh, it's just a rookie pilot," Wesley said absentmindedly, thinking what he'd really like to do would be to stick his whole head into the bucket of water to cool himself down. "They fly over all the time, looking just like that."

The plane coughed and farted a little trail of smoke.

"Nein," Günter spoke sharply. "I know the sound of a plane going down. My father took me flying. And," he added grimly, "I shot down enough Allied bombers to know."

That got Wesley's attention. He watched Günter look from the plane, coming closer and closer, to the men in the field, back to the plane—gauging something. The plane's motor hiccupped, off-on, off-on. "He hopes to emergency land here."

"What are you talking about?" Wesley asked.

Günter answered by grabbing Wesley by the arm. "Run!" he warned. He darted to Ron and Freddy, shoving them, too. "Run!"

"Get your mitts off me, you Nazi a-hole!" Ron shouted.

But Günter ignored him. He waved his arms, shouting at the other POWs at the far end of the field. *"Achtung! Achtung!"*

The POWs paused, hoes in hand, looking first toward Günter and then up toward the plane that was clearly in trouble. Wesley knew that he would never, ever, forget their reaction.

They cheered.

Looking horrified, Günter let his arms drop to his sides.

For a moment, everyone froze, not sure they were reading the POWs' reaction properly. But most Americans knew the German word *"dummkopf"* for "idiot" from Hollywood movies. So they could translate what the bullying German said next, *"Dummer Amerikaner!"* His companions laughed.

All hell broke loose then, starting with Charles. "You bloody bastards," he screamed, rushing the first POW he could get to. Bobby dashed to help him. So did Ron. Mr. Ratcliff ran to stop them.

The guard shot into the air, shouting, "Hold it right there! All of you!"

In the fray, no one noticed the plane's engine cut off altogether and the smoke streaming from the engine—no one except Günter and Wesley.

They spun around as the plane started whistling and dipped sharply on one wing. The pilot was clearly trying to bank away from the field where he could now see all these people, fighting and shouting.

In the same agonizing instance, Wesley recognized where the plane was pointed—straight at the twins!

It was another nightmare, it had to be, Wesley thought. This can't be happening. "Johnny! Jamie!" he shrieked.

At Wesley's call, they looked up from their butterflies. They stopped and stared at the plane.

Wesley forced his legs to run. "Johnny, Jamie!"

Günter was already sprinting flat out toward the children, shouting, "Look out! *Raus aus dem Weg!* Move!" But they didn't. They just stood, holding hands, little statues of confused fear.

Somehow Günter managed to scoop the twins up and dive out of the way, just as the plane hit the ground and started skidding out of control—right toward where Johnny and Jamie had stood just moments before.

Bouncing and lurching, the plane slid across the field. Then it tore through brambles, wheels squealing. It smashed into a walnut tree. The old tree heaved to one side with the impact, and an enormous branch cracked off to crash down onto the plane's nose with a thunderous bang.

Little licks of flame popped out of the engine. If it really ignited, it could set the tree ablaze, maybe even the entire grove around it.

Behind Wesley, Freddy started shouting. "It's gonna catch fire! Grandpop! Get water! Quick!"

"Dear God," murmured Wesley. He knew there were no fire trucks to contain a forest fire this far in the countryside. Last summer, a house near them had been struck by lightning and burned to the ground.

Then he had another sickening thought. The pilot!

Again, Günter was way ahead of Wesley, ahead of everybody. As the Ratcliffs rushed to lug buckets of water to the plane, Günter scrambled onto its running board. Yanking and tugging, he dragged the unconscious pilot out and onto the ground.

Just as the plane engine exploded into flames.

It took quite a while for the fire to be put out completely and for the air force ambulance to retrieve the pilot, who miraculously woke up with only a bad bump on his head. Only then did things calm down enough that Wesley could explain to Mr. Ratcliff that Günter had saved Johnny's and Jamie's lives. He and Freddy had been the only ones to witness it.

"I can't thank you enough, son," Mr. Ratcliff said, shaking Günter's hand over and over, gratitude softening his usual authoritative voice.

"A small act to balance out others," Günter answered quietly.

When Günter climbed up into the truck's flatbed with the other Germans to return to their POW camp for the night, Mr. Ratcliff closed the tailgate behind him. "I won't ever forget what you did here today," he said.

"Wir auch nicht," muttered the hulking Nazi sitting next to Günter.

Wesley waved as the truck pulled away. Günter had been the hero of the day. The air force captain who'd come to assess the plane's damage had even said he was going to write a story about Günter for the *Stars and Stripes* newspaper. He should be very proud of himself, thought Wesley. But all Günter seemed to be was nervous.

"Hey, Wes?" Freddy came up beside him as the POW truck disappeared around a bend. "You seen my map? I can't find it anywhere. I must have dropped it in the excitement."

Chapter Twenty-three

About eight o'clock that evening, Sheriff Bailey knocked on the Ratcliffs' door.

"Sorry to bother you, Andy, but two POWs in your work crew have run off. I was wondering if you might have some idea where they'd head."

"What? No. Come on in, Matthew." Mr. Ratcliff opened the screened door. The men stood in the hallway while all the boys crowded the living room doorway to listen.

"The POWs out on work details do this sometimes," explained the sheriff. "Mostly they just go for a stroll and turn themselves in after a few hours of playing hooky. Like they were tourists or something. It's the dangdest thing. But I don't think that's what happened with these two."

Wesley felt a sudden cold river of anxiety flush through him as he eavesdropped. What if that bully Nazi had found Freddy's map? He might be on his way to sabotage an important air force secret project! And it'd be his fault! He tugged on his brother's sleeve. "Charles, I may have done a bad thing."

Charles waved him off, listening to the sheriff.

"After leaving your farm, the driver pulled into Mike's station for gas. The guard let the POWs go inside while he bought himself a candy bar." He laughed in a snort. "I wouldn't want to be in that fellow's shoes tonight. The camp CO is pretty riled. Anyhoo, they all got back into the truck, except one."

Mr. Ratcliff nodded. "One of them was real trouble, Matthew, a Hitler diehard. Massive guy, stupid grin, nasty attitude. I can see him lighting out just to cause trouble. Know the one I mean?"

"I do. He caused quite a ruckus there at the station when the guard realized he'd lost one. The guy you're describing, a Corporal Krautwald, knocked the guard over and ran into the woods and got away."

"You're kidding me."

"Nope," the sheriff said. "Like I said, I think that guard's going to be on KP duty the rest of his life. No, the one who'd run off first was a little fellow." The sheriff opened up his notebook. "Hmmmm. A boy named Günter Schmitt."

"You don't say?" Mr. Ratcliff stuck out his lower lip out, thinking. "That boy's no Nazi, Matthew. He saved my youngest two today, and the pilot, when that trainee plane crash-landed in our fields. Fact is, I worried that fanatical Nazi corporal would jump on the chance to beat up that kid as fast as a duck jumps a june bug."

"Yup, I know. There's been some trouble at the camps with

Hitler true-believers terrorizing regular German soldiers. Plus, a few so-called suicides I wonder about."

Mr. Ratcliff let out a low whistle. "I wonder if that's why Günter ran off to begin with."

"Well." The sheriff put his hat back on. "I need to locate them both, fast. Got some boys helping me comb the woods. Like to come?"

"Let me get my rifle," Mr. Ratcliff answered.

"I'll come too," Bobby volunteered.

"No way, son." Mr. Ratcliff put his hand on Bobby's shoulder and pulled him aside so the sheriff couldn't hear. "They'll be a bunch of trigger-happy old-timers out to prove they're still patriots. I'm more worried about them than the POWs. You stay here and watch after your mama and Patsy. There was a Nazi who got away from Camp Pickett and attacked a woman in Burkeville before they caught him. Like I said, I can't imagine that boy Günter doing anything bad. But that other one?" He shook his head. "That one's full of hate."

"All right, troops." Bobby took over as soon as his father left. "Johnny, you stand post on the back porch with Ron. Jamie, you come up the drive with me to watch the road. Chuck, you and Wes patrol the barns." He took a shotgun from the closet and handed one to Charles and one to Ron. "Okay, men..."

"Hold on, boys!" Patsy stopped them. "You're overreacting a bit, aren't you? Two runaway POWs don't exactly make up an invasion force."

That finally gave Wesley the chance to speak up. "I think I know where one of them will go."

"Where's that?" asked Charles and Bobby at the same time.

"Well, you see . . ." He stalled, knowing his big brother would be furious at him for letting a Jerry capture a secret map. "Well, it's like this. Freddy told me about some hush-hush military project just east of the air base, at Elko. The army took over acres and acres of land to build *something*. We thought it might be a secret rocket project or something exciting, like in *Flash Gordon*." He shrugged. "We just wanted to see."

"Wesley, honey," Patsy interrupted gently. "What does that have to do with the POWs?"

"Oh, right-o. Well . . ." Wesley looked nervously from face to face. "Well, earlier today Freddy traced the route on a map to show me how to get there. But this afternoon, after all the hubbub, he couldn't find it. And . . . and . . . that POW Günter might have heard us talking about it."

"*God's teeth*, Wes!" Charles exploded. "You know the dangers of being a busybody! What if ninny-gnat gossips had snooped around the D-day troops hiding at Southampton? The invasion might have been completely spoilt. What if there's something really important being made at Elko and you've just handed that information to the Jerries?"

Wesley felt like he might burst into tears.

"Why didn't you tell the sheriff about this?" Bobby asked.

"I . . . I . . . I was too embarrassed."

"Well, it's too late now anyway," Bobby said, holding up his hand to stop Charles from exploding again. "They're gone. What do you think we should do, Chuck?"

Charles turned to Patsy. "When we were plane watching, didn't the Civilian Air Defense tell us we might see aircraft heading in that direction?"

She thought a moment. "You're right, they did. Mr. Ewell said there was something around Elko the air force would use for diversion in case of an attack on Richmond."

"We've got to head up there," Charles announced. "We've got to go right now. We've got to catch those Nazis. Come on! We'll be heroes!"

"Right!" Bobby clapped his hands together, like he did in a football huddle once he set the next play. "Wait a minute." He hesitated. "I promised Daddy that I'd guard the house and the womenfolk." He frowned with obvious disappointment.

"Humph." Patsy retreated into the kitchen and re-emerged holding a heavy cast-iron frying pan. She held it up with some menace. "As if Mama and I can't handle ourselves. She's a better shot with the rifle than you are, Bobby. I'll tell the twins I need their protection so they stay here out of trouble. Go on now. Shoo!"

"Lean over! I can't see!" Ron pushed Freddy to one side.

Freddy clung to the handlebars of Ron's bike as he sat on it and rested his back against Ron to keep from falling off. His legs dangled on either side of the front wheel. Wesley and Charles followed on another bike, with Bobby bringing up the rear, three rifles strapped to his back.

"Take this turn." Freddy pointed.

The boys leaned and swerved, top-heavy, onto White Oak Road.

"Almost there," he shouted.

Thank God, thought Wesley. He was sitting on handlebars too, and his butt was falling asleep, tingling with painful pinpricks. But he wasn't about to ask Charles to stop. His brother was pedaling like a madman. Even Bobby was starting to lag, but Charles pushed him on.

"Hurry! We've got to hurry," Charles urged, fighting against the burning pain in his own legs.

Finally, he had the chance to do something to avenge his homeland, his school chums, his neighbors. Finally, he had a way to make up for his stupidity in running away and then getting so sick. He'd catch those accursed German POWs and bring them to justice. The Ratcliffs would be seen as heroes. He'd bring honor, not embarrassment, to them.

Just like the night he'd run away, a silvery full moon glittered in the black sky. But unlike that disastrous night, no clouds were gathering. The stars shone brightly, like a heavenly candelabra of light. The boys could see easily up the dirt road.

"Train tracks ahead," Freddy called. "Stop here."

Bobby, Charles, and Ron skidded to a halt. Freddy and Wesley climbed off the bars, rubbing their butts.

"There was a guard over the tracks last time I was here," Freddy whispered. "But I don't see anyone now."

"We better split up," said Bobby, "to cover ground faster. Isn't there a swamp and a creek over the other side of the tracks?"

Freddy nodded. "The soldiers put down a log bridge over the creek."

"Okay, men," ordered Bobby. "We'll cross and then fan out. Let's go!"

The sound of their footsteps on the rough log bridge was completely covered by the high-pitched chorus of spring peepers in the swamp's inky waters. There must be thousands of them, thought Wesley. He waved his arms against the mosquitoes that whined in swarms around his ears, accidentally whacking Ron.

"Move over!" Ron elbowed him.

"Shhhhhh!" Bobby and Charles shushed him.

Once on the other side, Bobby and Ron turned right to search east. Charles, Wesley, and Freddy split off and headed west.

Within minutes, Charles could see a clearing ahead through the forest. He signaled Wesley and Freddy to creep forward, tree by tree. The boys came to a wide, open field. In the middle of it were two flat, long, dirt lanes. Runways!

"I told you so!" Freddy said.

Across the landing field were the silhouettes of fifteen fighter-size planes. But everything was still and silent, like a ghost town.

"This is weird," Charles whispered. "Where are the airmen? The ground crew?"

Wesley pointed to several barrack huts and a fleet of trucks. Netting covered what looked like mounted machine guns. "Maybe over there?"

"Let's go see," Charles answered. The three boys snuck along the edge of the clearing. Suddenly Wesley gasped and pointed.

Dashing across the field toward the planes was the shadow of a person.

Oh yes! Charles's heart pounded with excitement. He raised his rifle and tracked the runner's path. "Slow down, Nazi!" he muttered. "Slow down enough that I can take a good shot."

"What are you doing?" Wesley cried. "It could be an American."

Charles kept his eye to the rifle sight. "Running like that? Not likely." He cocked the rifle, centering the racing figure in his crosshairs. Is this what Nazi Stuka pilots felt, Charles wondered, as they strafed civilians running away in panic along the ground? Is this what Luftwaffe bomber crews felt as they pulled the lever to drop death on a sleeping city?

Charles's hands started to shake.

Wesley tugged on his sleeve. "Charles, don't!"

Charles hesitated. Bringing the POWs back was the plan, he argued with himself. Bringing them back so the Ratcliff family would get credit for capturing them. That would mean *alive*. Biting his lip, Charles lowered the gun. "He's gotten to the planes. Come on!"

The boys darted across the runways and threw themselves behind a truck. Crouching, Charles crawled to its bumper to peep around its front. He could hear the POW yanking and tugging, the slip and slide of camouflage netting being pulled off a plane.

He turned back to Wesley to say he was going to rush the

bum, and put his hand on the truck to push himself into standing upright. The truck wobbled at his touch. Startled, Charles looked closer. The truck had no headlights. He tapped it. It rattled. Good grief! The truck was made of plywood! It was a . . .

"Falschung!" the German cried out in despair. *"Nein, Nein! Verdammt. Das Flugzeug ist eine Falschung? Was soll ich tun?"*

"Guess the planes are fake, too." Charles muttered, judging the disappointment in the POW's voice. He must have thought he could fly out of Virginia. Charles laughed ruefully, recognizing the whole airfield had to be a decoy—a trick to confuse enemy aircrew and lure them away from Richmond's bases and war plants. Well, it'd certainly fooled one German and a bunch of kids, hadn't it?

"Stay here," Charles told Wesley and Freddy. He stepped out from behind the make-believe truck and, holding his rifle high, slowly approached the German runaway.

The POW was bent over, hands on his knees, crying. He didn't seem to know Charles was there.

"Hands up, mate," Charles ordered.

The German jumped back in surprise. It was Günter. For a moment he just stared at Charles.

"Hands up!" Charles repeated.

Günter shook his head, his blond hair shining in the moonlight. "*Nein*. I cannot go back. They will kill me at the camp."

"Can't say I care, mate," Charles answered, ice in his voice.

Günter shook his head again. "I am sorry," he said quietly, "but I cannot surrender."

He bolted.

"Stop!" Charles bellowed after him.

But Günter didn't. He raced back toward the swamp.

Charles ran after him. Wesley and Freddy followed. Soon Charles was way ahead, all those runs he'd made on the football field making him far faster than the younger boys. Come on, he urged himself.

He heard the German youth jump into the water and thrash through it. Now I've got him, Charles thought. The water will slow him down. Charles could see the swampy creek just ahead. Günter was waist-deep in the water.

"St—" he started to shout again, when he heard Günter scream in pain and back up to the shore, thrashing madly.

Charles slid to a stop at the edge of the muddy bank. Günter was writhing on the ground, clutching his leg, as a four-foot-long black shadow of a snake slithered away.

Chapter Twenty-four

"Nerts," said Freddy, as he and Wesley caught up, panting, just in time to see the snake slide into the water and swim away. "That's one big-daddy water moccasin. That Nazi boy can die from that bite."

Günter moaned and rolled on the ground.

Charles stared at him. Just as Wesley's mind had often betrayed him, throwing him back to their nightmare Atlantic crossing, Charles's memories suddenly shoved him back in time, to another scene of someone in pain. Another moment that he had frozen, not knowing what to do. His mind leaped to England, to the aftermath of a Luftwaffe raid, when their neighbor had writhed and sobbed on the ground until the Home Guard carried him away on a stretcher, his legs mangled by his own chimney falling on him.

"Charles! We've got to do something!" Wesley cried. "What's wrong with you? He saved the twins, remember?"

Charles looked up abruptly, as Wesley's voice yanked him out of the nightmare memory. He shook his head ever so slightly to collect himself. "Right. Someone needs to go for help."

"There's a general store at the crossroad," said Freddy. "Storekeeper lives in the back. I suspect they have a telephone in the store."

"Is it close?"

"About two miles."

"You two take my bike and go," Charles said.

"Carrying two bodies slows down a bicycle," Freddy said. "I'll do it alone."

Wesley caught Freddy's arm. "Didn't you tell me it can be dangerous for you to be out really late on your own?"

"Oh yeah, some places. But I know most people along this stretch of road. They're good folk. I've been jerking your chain some, Wes. Fact is, I've come to trust white men more being around you and the Ratcliffs. Even old Ron's growing on me. I'll just sing out as I come to the store what my errand is, 'cause the storekeeper might suppose a Negro boy on a bike at night is there to rob him. Just like I figured you were trouble when you showed up just as night was falling at Gran's house that first time.

"Plus, here's the main thing. You *limeys*,"—he grinned as he said it—"sure don't know the way." He straightened up. "If I get to be a hero along with y'all, I gotta do my part."

He pointed to Günter. "Put that boy's leg below his heart so the poison doesn't travel up to it." Then Freddy disappeared into the gloom of the trees.

"Come on, Wes, help me lay him out straight." Charles spoke to Günter: "We've got to move you a bit."

"Leave me," Günter protested. "I rather die here. Not hanged in the barrack outhouse by *Lager-Gestapo*."

"Listen, pops," Charles snapped. "I don't much care whether you live or die. But if you die, it's not going to be because we stood by and did nothing. It's not how things are done here in America." He'd learned that much from the Ratcliffs, anyway.

Günter groaned as Charles and Wesley pulled him up the embankment so he lay on an incline, his head and chest higher than his leg.

"Golly, Charles," murmured Wesley, "his leg is ballooning up fast. Look at it." Just below his knee, Günter's leg was already the size of a small cantaloupe. "What should we do?"

It wasn't like Charles had a lot of experience with snakebites. "Better get a look at what we're dealing with," he answered. He pulled out his pocketknife and cut open Günter's pant leg.

They both gasped at how red and swollen Günter's calf was. There were two large holes in the skin where the snake's fangs had punctured it and shot in venom. The holes oozed blood, and the skin surrounding them glowed with yellow bile.

"God's teeth," Charles muttered. Remembering that Freddy had warned they shouldn't let the poison travel to Günter's heart, he cut a strip of cloth from Günter's pants and tied it tight, just above his kneecap. The first-aid training all British children received during the Blitz told him to pull it tight enough that

his finger could still slip under the cloth. Tie it too tight and the German POW could lose his leg if he did live.

Charles sat back on his heels, not knowing what else to do.

Günter reached up and grasped Charles's sleeve. "I need to confess, in case . . . in case I die."

"What are you talking about? I'm no priest."

Günter ignored him. "I lied about being drafted. I wish to say why. Because"—he tugged on Charles's sleeve—"you remind me of me."

"What the hell!" Charles tried to pull his arm away. "I'm nothing like you."

Günter stubbornly held on. "I live in Lübeck, on the Baltic Sea. It was full of timber-framed houses, like Stratford-upon-Avon."

"You've been to England?" Charles asked with surprise.

"Oh yes. My father loved Shakespeare. He took us."

Günter flinched and shifted, clearly in pain. He looked past Charles, up to the sky. "It was a beautiful night like this that your RAF came to destroy Lübeck. Our bay shone bright with moonlight. It lit up the city for your bombardiers to see. The city had a small U-boat building yard. But mostly we were peaceful. We had little air defense."

He shook his head. "The RAF raid set all the old wooden houses aflame. *Meine mutter*. . ." He choked on the words and his face puckered. "My mother died as she tried to pull my young sisters from the inferno. I tried to help but . . ." He drifted off, tears glistening on his face.

After a moment, he continued, his voice trembling, "Lübeck was the first German city your RAF bombed in large numbers with incendiaries. Our radio told us Churchill bragged and said it showed Hitler the RAF could penetrate German territory."

Listening, Charles felt a strange mix of guilt, pride, and vindication. What did this German expect after the Luftwaffe had set half of London on fire?

Günter nodded, seeming to read Charles's expression. "I joined the Luftwaffe to avenge my family. I wanted to kill many British. Like you do Germans. I was too young to be a pilot. Sixteen years. They put me on flak guns. When I hit my first Allied bomber, it exploded. My unit took me drinking to celebrate. I was sick afterward. But not from beer."

Günter's blue eyes closed, his grip started to loosen. But then he roused himself and asked, "Have you read *The Merchant of Venice*?"

Charles nodded. But why the devil was the Nazi bringing up Shakespeare?

"The city's Christians shame the Jewish merchant, remember?" Günter paused, waiting for Charles to nod that he did. "I have been thinking about what the merchant tells them. I played him for my school production. It seems so long ago now. Happier times." Günter paused, closing his eyes to remember: "The merchant says, 'If you wrong us, shall we not revenge?' Then he promises, 'The villainy you teach me, I will execute. . . . But I will better the instruction.'" Günter tugged on Charles's sleeve once more. "We taught you villainy. Now you teach us. Your D-day is the beginning of the true lesson."

The boys were silent for a moment. Charles remembered

Murrow's description of the RAF raid on Berlin as *an orchestrated hell—a terrible symphony of light and flame.*

Günter let go of Charles, falling back onto the ground. He smiled weakly. "I heard you talk in the fields. Go home, yes. Defend it. Kill if you must to serve your country. But revenge is a poison. Like this snake. Fight to end hatred. Fight to bring peace. Yes?"

Charles frowned. Then he slowly nodded.

Günter turned to look at Wesley. "I wish I met your Indian." His voice was fading. "Take my book. It tells of two enemies—a white man and an Apache—coming to respect each other, becoming friends. Perhaps like us, yes?" Günter's head drooped to one side.

Wesley gasped. "Is he dead?"

Charles put his head against Günter's chest and listened. "No, his heart is still beating." He sat up. Günter's mention of Apaches had reminded Charles of something. "Wes, were you there the day Mr. Johns's dog was bitten by a snake?"

"No!"

"I'm trying to remember what he did. For starters, I'm going to have to cut open the snake punctures and suck out the poison."

"Oh, Charles!" Wesley's eyes got big. "Can't that make you sick too?"

Grimly, he nodded. "I need to be jolly well careful." He paused, holding up his little knife as he thought. "Mr. Johns did something else, too. He used the roots of some weed; it had little yellow flowers. Any idea what that was?"

"I do! Mr. Johns said it was the one good thing we British did for them. We brought Saint-John's-wort in our ships because it could treat wounds. It's gone native here. It grows all over."

"Do you know what it looks like?"

"Oh yes! He showed me. Oh, this is so exciting, Charles! We'll be like medicine men!"

"Wes, for God's sake, be serious. This isn't make-believe. Can you find some, quick?"

Wesley sobered. "It should grow along the creek."

"Go look. But be careful. Watch for more snakes. I'm going to bring up some mud so we can mix a kind of poultice with the two. Hurry!"

The brothers snapped into the same life-or-death focus they'd learned during air raids in England. Charles dug up fistfuls of dense, wet mud. Wesley scurried and found a batch of flowering, three-foot-tall Saint-John's-wort. The ground was so wet he easily yanked up several by their roots. He raced back to Charles.

"Brilliant!" said Charles. He cut the roots into wedges like apple slices and handed one to Wesley. "Chew this up. Make it the consistency of a pudding. All right? Once I've drawn out the poison, you spit that glop out and pack it on the wound. Then we cover that with mud. Got it?"

Wesley wrinkled his nose and nearly threw up at the root's earthy taste. But he chewed, his mouth filling with a syrupy paste he was careful not to swallow.

"Here goes," Charles muttered as he put the knife's blade against Günter's skin, just below the puncture holes. Not too deep, he cautioned himself. Just enough to release the venom. Like prying out a big splinter. *For pity's sake, stop blithering and do it!*

Charles clasped his two hands together to stop their shaking. He punctured the skin and cut a shallow inch-long line. Günter moaned as the wound erupted, pus and blood streaming down his calf.

Now to draw out the poison. Charles took a deep breath. It's now or never, Bishop, he thought. For the first time in a long while, the Lord's Prayer filled Charles's mind and heart: "Forgive us our trespasses as we . . ."—he paused and emphasized the words to himself—*"as we forgive those who trespass against us."*

Chapter Twenty-five

"Eeeeewwww!" Jamie and Johnny squealed in delighted disgust. "Did you really suck out snake venom?" "Did you really chew up a smelly old root?" "Really?" "Did you really?"

Charles smiled mysteriously and took a bite of his pancake, not answering. Wesley followed his lead, thoroughly enjoying their new status as family legends.

"Yes, they did, boys," said Mr. Ratcliff as he sat down at the kitchen table with a cup of coffee. He'd been outside talking with the sheriff while the boys ate. "And don't you ever think about doing something like that, because it could kill you. And if it didn't kill you, I'd tan your behinds." But he winked at Charles as he said it.

"What did Sheriff Bailey say, Dad?" Bobby asked.

"Well, sir, as we speak, Günter is being transported to Fort Eustis in Newport News. Evidently, at that camp the army is going to teach more open-minded Germans the principles of democratic government with the hope they will lead Germany to a better way of doing things after the war. On the flip side, the Kraut we old men caught is being sent to Oklahoma to a die-hard Nazi camp where there's maximum security."

Mr. Ratcliff rocked back in his chair. "Now, here's the real excitement. Charles and Wesley are going to be written up in the *Richmond Times-Dispatch*. The sheriff's calling them true red-white-and-blue *American* heroes."

"What?" Charles and Wesley asked together.

"I reminded him that you two are British. He thought that made the story even better."

"Hold your horses," said Ron. "Bobby and me went looking for that guy too, you know."

"Aww, come on, Ron," Bobby started to silence him.

But Wesley interrupted. "We wouldn't have gotten there without Freddy either. He told us where to go, and Freddy wouldn't have been there if you hadn't given him a ride on your bike, Ron. We'll tell the newspaper that, won't we, Charles?"

"Yeah, that's right," Ron said, nodding and sitting up taller. Then he grinned and added, "Limey."

The boys laughed and went back to their pancakes.

Patsy rolled her eyes. "Honestly, don't you boys ever tire of goosing one another?" She turned to Charles. "I'm just glad you're all right. What you did was very brave. And kind."

It was the first time she'd really looked at him since getting the news that Henry was missing in action. Charles felt a little twinge of that suppressed crush on her.

There was a knock on the door.

"Goodness," sighed Mrs. Ratcliff. "What now?" She got up to answer it.

"Probably the newspaper people," Mr. Ratcliff explained. "The sheriff said they wanted a photograph of you two. Better finish your food and go clean up."

"Yeah, gotta get pretty for the cameras," Bobby teased.

Mrs. Ratcliff came back into the kitchen. She held a telegram. Her face was pale.

"What is it, Mary Lee?"

She answered by approaching Charles and putting her hand on his shoulder. "It's from your mama, honey. She's fine. But your daddy has been hurt. He was at church with your uncle, the Buckingham Palace guard, when some new kind of Nazi bomb came out of the blue and hit the Guard's Chapel, completely destroying it during Sunday service. It's an unmanned rocket bomb, of all things. No planes needed, so there was no air raid warning sounded. Those poor people saying their prayers didn't know trouble was coming. Hitler's calling it V-something. Some German word for vengeance. It's nothing but pure spite."

Mrs. Ratcliff knelt by the table to catch Wesley up in a hug. "Sugar, I'm so sorry. Your uncle is dead. The roof collapsed on him and about two hundred other people." She hurried to add, "Thank the good Lord that your daddy was pulled out alive. His legs and hip were broken. But your daddy will recuperate. It'll just take time and considerable bed rest.

"Wesley, you'll stay here with us. Charles"—Mrs. Ratcliff turned to back to him—"your mama says she needs your help to take care of your dad. These days, the Atlantic crossing is safer. Our navy has the upper hand on the seas. She wants you to come on home now."

"All ashore that's going ashore!" a merchant sailor called, in the last call for boarding.

The time had come.

Charles glanced over his shoulder at the Liberty ship, crammed with wartime cargo for England, that he was about to board. Finally, he was going home as he'd longed to do. But he was leaving America, which he had come to love too. He hadn't expected how bittersweet the parting would feel.

"Well, this is it." He smiled and shrugged uncomfortably, turning back to the Ratcliffs there to see him off. "Please tell Ed for me that I really appreciate his son arranging a berth for me on his boat."

Mr. Ratcliff nodded. "I will."

"And, Mr. Ratcliff, I can't thank you enough . . . for everything."

"It's been a pleasure, son. You be careful now, you hear?"

Charles nodded and stepped to face Bobby.

Awkwardly, Bobby punched Charles's shoulder. Charles punched him back.

"Hey," Bobby joked. "That's my throwing arm!" Then his face grew sad. "The football team just won't be the same without you, Chuck."

Charles swallowed. "Nawww, it'll be okay. Ron's coming up next year. Bet he can catch your passes. They're always spot-on. Right, Ron?"

Ron grinned that new genuine smile of his. "That's right... old chum." He shook Charles's hand.

Bobby grabbed Charles in a bear hug, the two friends slapping each other's back.

Patsy was next.

"I'll never forget how you encouraged me about my artwork," she said in a low voice. "Maybe I'll come to London someday to see all the paintings you described. Buy me a cup of coffee if I do?"

"Tea," Charles corrected her. *God's teeth! What a stupid good-bye!* But it was too late to say anything else as Patsy kissed him on the cheek, and stepped back to let him say his good-byes to Wesley.

The two Bishop brothers had already discussed their parting. No blithering at the dock, they'd agreed. Now they faced each other in a kind of attention, even though tears blurred their eyes.

Charles took his little brother's arm by the elbow. "Stiff upper lip, now."

"Never show we're downhearted." Wesley repeated the mantra the brothers had been told as they'd boarded the ship that took them to the States, across the treacherous, wide waters of the Atlantic, three thousand miles from home, not knowing if there would even be an England for them to return to one day.

"Good little ambassadors for England," Charles finished.

Wesley nodded.

"Good lad," Charles said. "Do write me what is going on here. Just like we did for Mum and Dad, eh?"

"Shore 'nough," Wesley drawled in a perfect Tidewater Virginia accent.

Charles laughed, proud of his little brother's new shield of humor. He started to turn.

"Charles," Wesley whispered.

"Yes?"

"There's a stowaway in your bag."

"What?"

"My stuffed koala bear. I haven't had nightmares for the longest time now. And I'm going to move in with Ron and the twins since you're leaving. Ron and I talked about it. Bobby should take the attic bedroom. Ron said I can hang Churchill and our model Spitfires over my bed. So I don't need Joey anymore." He smiled and added with a new Charles-like swagger, "And since I can't be on the ship to look after you properly, Joey can."

"Glad you told me, Wes, so I didn't unpack him around a bunch of sailors!"

"Be careful, Charles. Old Adolf's still out there, you know."

Charles squeezed Wesley's arm. Then he gave the Ratcliffs one last fond look. He'd learned so much from them—about friendship, about generosity, about standing up to trouble. "Right-o," he said. "I'm off."

Putting his British bravado back on like a life jacket, Charles stepped onto the gangplank.

From an adjacent ship, docked and unloading, a sailor shouted. He threw up his arms in greeting. Then he raced down the gangplank to gather up a beautiful girl waiting there for him with a Hollywood-perfect kiss. It was the kind of unabashed display of joy Yanks were so good at, Charles thought as he watched, the kind of spontaneity and openness he'd come to really appreciate. He'd have to try to hold on to that American influence back home in England, that uninhibited courage to say what they honestly thought and felt.

Wait a minute. Charles stopped in his tracks. What did he have to lose? He dropped his bag. He turned and strode down the gangplank—straight for Patsy.

Before she could protest, he grabbed her. He wrapped his arms around her. And he kissed those lips he'd longed to touch. It was his very first kiss. And it was beautiful. He'd remember the sweet burning press of it for the rest of his life.

Mr. Ratcliff cleared his throat loudly.

Charles let go and imitated the thickest of London cockney accents. "That's what you missed out on, love."

With that and an enormous self-satisfied grin, Charles swaggered back up the gangplank. As he stepped onto the ship's steel deck, an Andrews Sisters tight-harmony hit filled his mind. It was one of those American big band, swing-dance melodies, the kind during which a boy could dazzle a girl with a dip and a slide, and then grab her for a whirling embrace. The song was all about confident, no-regret good-byes as a man sailed off to sea. *Don't cry, baby. . . . Shhh-shoo baby, shoo, shoo.*

Charles crossed the deck to face the ocean as the sailors released the ship's mooring ropes. Its foghorn blared farewell, and the boat skimmed out into the Chesapeake Bay currents. The sun was warm. The sky was clear. The waters were calm and beckoning, a gray-blue mirror of the azure heavens. Charles knew he was heading back into uncertainties, back into a war-tossed world. But he was ready to face it now, to fight, as Günter had advised—not for revenge—but to stop those who brought war and delighted in it.

Charles took in a deep breath of salty air. It smelled like home. It smelled of promise.

Back on the docks, the Ratcliff boys stared at Patsy. Flustered, blushing, she laughed out loud. “What a cheeky bloke!” she murmured, touching her lips.

Wesley smiled to himself. It was the very first time Wesley had ever heard Patsy use a British phrase. It’d be the first thing he’d write Charles.

Afterword

"All the great things are simple, and many can be expressed in a single word: freedom, justice, honor, duty, mercy, hope."—Winston Churchill

In May 1940, Hitler's Blitzkrieg (lightning war) gobbled up nation after nation with terrifying ease. Denmark fell in one day, Holland in five, Belgium in eighteen, and France in six weeks. Only Great Britain remained standing in defiance.

Immediately, Hitler's Luftwaffe set up air bases along France's coast, just across the English Channel. It took Nazi bombers a mere sixteen minutes to be over London. In contrast, the British RAF needed eleven minutes to scramble their fighter planes—once they knew the Luftwaffe was coming. At first, the RAF had only seven hundred serviceable planes to fight the Luftwaffe's thirty-five hundred. "Never was so much owed by so many to so few," Prime Minister Churchill said about the pilots who raced up into the sky to face down the Luftwaffe legions.

The Blitz—Hitler's air campaign to pound the British into surrendering—began in earnest on September 7, 1940, when the Luftwaffe dropped nearly a hundred tons of incendiary bombs on London. After that, Nazi bombers came almost nightly. With each raid, hundreds of homes went up in flames.

To survive, the British huddled in deep Tube (subway) stations and prefab backyard bomb shelters. Cardboard boxes containing gas masks hung from their necks at all times. Barrage balloons and ack-ack cannons ringed the city. Thousands became volunteer firemen, ambulance drivers, or simply joined the effort each morning to dig out their neighbors from rubble. More than 43,000 British civilians died, including 7,736 children.

Most children were sent out of the cities to the relatively safer countryside. But when the Blitz started, the American embassy was besieged with two thousand frantic calls a day from parents wanting their sons and daughters out of England entirely. About four thousand children came to the United States, some sponsored by the CORB (Children's Overseas Reception Board), their costs paid for by the British government. After ten days, however, that board had stopped taking applications—they'd already received 211,448 pleas for the few thousand slots they had to offer.

As ships steamed out of Liverpool for dangerous two-week crossings, evacuee children sang "There Will Always Be an England." From July to October 1940, the height of the evacuations, German U-boat submarines (*Unterseeboot*) sunk 217 British ships. To safeguard them, children's ships were tucked into large convoys sailing in zigzags. Portholes were blacked out and screwed shut so no telltale shard of light shone along the waters. Children were strapped into cumbersome, orange cork life jackets.

Evacuee memoirs recount the fun they had—sailors taking them into the navigation cabin, and massive games of tag. But many were horrendously seasick and frightened. One child watched eleven of the twenty-eight ships in his convoy go under. Another survived dud torpedoes ricocheting harmlessly off his ship.

Then, tragically, in bad weather and high seas, the *City of Benares*, carrying ninety children, was torpedoed by U-48. Many children died in the explosion. Some fell into the sea as lifeboat pulleys jammed, tipping the boats. Other lifeboats capsized in the typhoonlike wake of the enormous ship as it went under. The convoy continued on, under orders to do so. The nearest British destroyer took nineteen hours to get there through a gale and hailstones. The crew reportedly wept when they found boats filled with dead children, a few survivors clinging to rafts.

One family lost all five of its children that night. Only thirteen youngsters survived, including the six CORB boys Charles thinks of as he struggles against the James River. The *Benares* tragedy brought an abrupt end to Britain's transatlantic evacuation of its children.

After the war, U-48's captain was tried for war crimes. Responsible for sinking fifty-five ships, he was put on trial specifically regarding the *Benares*. Nothing had marked the *Benares* as a children's ark. Outfitted with a large antisubmarine gun, she could be interpreted as a troop transport or military supply ship. The captain was acquitted, his actions deemed "within the rules of engagement."

Throughout World War II, a few U-boats did help survivors of the ships they torpedoed, giving them food and water, or even taking them on board, as did U-156 and Captain Werner Hartenstein after sinking a passenger ship, the *Laconia*. But, tragically, there were no international requirements that U-boats do so.

The British evacuees who made it typically relished their time in the States. Freed of gas masks and dark, long nights trembling in shelters, listening anxiously to the thud and bang of an aerial bombardment, they rediscovered childhood. They delighted in ice cream, hot showers, co-ed schools, Fourth of July homespun parades, and the unrestrained friendliness of most Americans. They marveled at our abundance of food, the suddenness and range of weather in the States plus its vastness, Frigidaires and ice cubes, jazz and blues, peanut butter and BLT sandwiches, toasted marshmallows, watermelons, and how small the White House was by comparison to Buckingham Palace.

They were disappointed not to meet Native Americans, cowboys, mobsters, or movie stars. But they heartily adopted American slang, dances, and mannerisms, and came to speak their minds with adults in a way that would shock their more formal British parents back home. Even so, evacuees often struggled to fit in. Isolationists embarrassed them by blaming the British for pulling the United States into war again. They were baffled by regional accents or sayings, and words having very different meanings. "Pants," for instance, in England meant "underwear."

Many felt guilty, and worried that their friends thought them "chicken" for leaving. Others, like my fictional Wesley, suffered what we now know as PTSD (post-traumatic stress disorder). They wet their beds, suffered bad dreams, and worried about their parents, especially since letters from home could take two months to arrive. Ironically, letters could spark nightmares. Accustomed to the Blitz, parents often spoke nonchalantly of terrifying events. One father matter-of-factly described his family's favorite pub being obliterated by a bomb, the blast near and strong enough to blow the shaving brush out of his hand.

U-boats, the American Merchant Marine, Shipbuilding, and Segregation

While the Luftwaffe bombed London, the German navy torpedoed incoming supplies—equipment, food, gas, and medicines—that kept England on its feet to fight. Called "gray wolves," the U-boat submarines skimmed along the water's surface at seventeen knots, much faster than cargo ships' average speed. They easily tracked convoys by spotting clouds of steam from smokestacks, or trails of discarded garbage.

When Hitler's U-boats turned their periscopes on the U.S. East Coast, they announced their threatening presence by German newspapers running a close-up photograph of Manhattan taken from a U-boat's conning tower. In the first eight months of 1942, a mere five Nazi U-boats managed to sink 397 freighters and tankers along our Atlantic coast.

Suddenly at war on two seas, our U.S. Navy could offer little protection. Tankers and freighters sailed unescorted, equipped with vintage guns from the First World War, their untrained, civilian watchmen searching the ocean for a tiny enemy periscope. German U-boat commanders, on the other hand, had easy viewing of our ships. Ignoring British warnings, we didn't mandate nighttime blackouts until May, meaning cargo ships sailing along our coast were backlit by a bright horizon of city lights. Nazi U-boat crews dubbed it "the great American turkey shoot."

Cape Hatteras, North Carolina, became nicknamed Torpedo Junction. Outer Banks residents kept kerosene by their back doors to wipe from their shoes the oil that covered the beaches from exploded tankers.

They grimly joked they could read at night by the glow of the ships burning off shore. They raked the sand every night and checked it each morning for footprints, to make sure no U-boat put saboteurs ashore as one managed to do in Florida. The account Wesley gives of Virginia Beach sunbathers witnessing four ships explode as they ran into a string of magnetic mines left by a U-boat the night before is true.

In the end, 1,554 American merchant ships were sunk and 9,521 mariners killed. According to USMM.org (American Merchant Marine at War), civilian sailors suffered the highest casualty rate of any service in World War II. One in eight experienced his ship going down. Yet they still joined. Their ranks quadrupled as they bravely delivered the critical supplies that kept Allied forces fighting.

A 1940s recruiting poster features a rough-hewn merchant mariner with a determined grimace on his face. The headline? "YOU BET I'M GOING BACK TO SEA!" Many of these volunteers, aged sixteen to seventy-eight, were African American. The merchant marine was the first racially integrated service.

Part of what finally stopped U-boats was the United States producing ships at an enormous speed. Just down the James River from the Ratcliffs' imaginary home was one of the country's busiest shipbuilding centers. Between 1942 and 1945, the Newport News Shipbuilding and Dry Dock Company built forty-seven fighting ships, including nine aircraft carriers like the *Ticonderoga.*

Cargo boats, called Liberty ships, were designed to be built in large numbers in the shortest time possible—welded rather than riveted together, reducing construction to thirty-five days. Welding could be taught quickly. Demand for such labor skyrocketed. Many African American workers won their first mainstream industrial jobs in newly integrated assembly lines. Some Liberty ships were even named for African American mariners lost to German torpedoes. The SS *William Cox,* for instance, honored an African American fireman who died on the *Atwater,* the same cargo ship on which Freddy's fictitious uncle dies.

All this while the country clung to segregation laws that mandated separate schools, water fountains, bathrooms, and seating on buses for black people. (To be accurate to the 1940s, my characters say "Negro" or "colored" rather than "African American" and "Indian" rather than "Native American.") Congress did not pass civil rights legislation until the 1960s, but the courage and dedication of African Americans during World War II—civilian and military—went a long way to hasten those laws.

Native Americans faced similar inequalities. In the 1940s, Virginia residents could only check off "white" or "colored" on documents such as birth certificates, so tribes ceased to legally exist. Native Americans' segregated schooling ended at the eighth grade. The only way for them to achieve a high school diploma was to go to a boarding school in Muskogee, Oklahoma.

And yet, Native Americans enlisted to fight, just as African Americans volunteered for legendary units like the all-black Tuskegee Airmen—fighter plane squadrons credited with saving hundreds of bomber crews from Luftwaffe attack. Navaho became important code talkers, using their native language to transmit messages during some of the Pacific's worst battles. The Japanese were never able to decode it.

Secret Air Bases

Also in the Richmond-Norfolk area was the Hampton Roads Port of Embarkation, which handled hundreds of thousands of U.S. troops heading to North Africa or Europe, processed POWs, and rushed D-day casualties to Richmond's McGuire Hospital. Tons of military supplies left its docks each month. January 5, 1944—the night several squadrons of the famed African American Tuskegee Airmen shipped out—was typical of its daily traffic. Convoy UGS.29 departed, taking sixty-three cargo ships and tankers, seventeen escort vessels, and nine troop transports carrying 6,067 fighting men.

Scattered between Norfolk and Richmond were more than a dozen military bases plus many war factories, producing things like Jeep tires, flak jackets, radar-baffling devices, parachutes, ship anchors, and jungle hammocks. Because of such critical activity, Elko was built just east of Richmond by the 936th Camouflage Battalion. Its soldiers cleared swamps, bulldozed in runways, and constructed dummy airplanes, antiaircraft guns, and barracks out of plywood and canvas. If Hitler managed to launch an aerial attack from carriers off our coast, Richmond's lights would shut off, while the fake airfield's lit up, hopefully tricking Luftwaffe bombers into dropping their loads harmlessly on the decoy.

Elko remained a hush-hush project even after the war, with locals speculating on all sorts of clandestine activities. It's likely the FBI, CIA, and National Guard conducted training there until it was sold to commercial development.

German POWS in America

Across the United States, 371,683 Germans were imprisoned in five hundred camps. POWs helped pick crops, log, and repair roads, and worked in nonwar factories like peanut-processing plants. Occasionally, they engaged in disruptive protest—scratching swastikas into peaches they picked in Virginia, for instance—but mostly their labor helped the United States when so many Americans were overseas fighting.

Only 1,583 escape attempts were *recorded.* The United States was vast and the POW camps rather luxurious, their food and housing equal to what our military provided its own personnel. POWs were offered college-level courses. Camps had libraries, soccer games, and art facilities, and allowed prisoners to carve puppets or plant gardens. The motivation to escape was small. Most escapes were as Sheriff Bailey describes to the Ratcliffs—sightseeing jaunts for a few hours.

Within the camps, however, die-hard Nazis did terrorize moderate Germans who they felt didn't adequately revere Hitler. The worst perpetuators were Rommel's elite *Afrika Korps*, ardent believers in Aryan superiority, shipped from African battlefields directly to the United States. They never saw German cities bombed or the Allied assault of Normandy's beaches. They dismissed such reports as American propaganda, and German prisoners recounting them as liars.

Any fraternization—listening to jazz or saying grits were tasty or befriending American guards—could bring the wrath of the *Lager-Gestapo* or "Holy Ghost." Offenders were warned by chicken bones in their bunks or were beaten in the latrine. There was a suspicious number of "suicides"—German soldiers hanged, suicide notes pinned to them confessing disloyalty to the fatherland.

Detecting such intimidation tactics was complicated by the fact that few American guards spoke German. But as reports of violence reached Washington, the United States separated Nazi fanatics into higher security facilities and offered more open-minded German POWs—like my character Günter—courses in democratic principles.

V-1 Rockets

Hitler's response to D-day was to launch the V-1 flying bomb, a pilotless jet-engine monoplane with a 150-mile range and one-ton warhead, like that described by Charles and Wesley's mother. *V* stood for "*Vergeltungswaffen*" or "vengeance." Their explosions were terrifyingly random, as rockets plummeted to earth wherever their engines cut off. Londoners froze upon hearing the V-1's telltale *putt-putting* hum, waiting for the silence that signaled its fall. Blasts were enormous. Windows as far away as a quarter of a mile would shatter.

At their height, the V-1s destroyed twenty thousand houses a day. The V-2s were even deadlier and faster, unstoppable once launched. More than three thousand Allied flyers sacrificed their lives to bomb those launchpads, their locations discovered by unnamed French Resistance heroes.

Odds and Ends

CBS correspondent Edward R. Murrow rode on twenty-four bombing runs during World War II. He survived to host TV news back in the States after the war. Jock Abercrombie, however, the pilot of *D-Dog*, was killed a month after taking Murrow to the "Orchestrated Hell" the Ratcliff family listens to on their radio.

Günter's favorite author, Karl May, is still beloved in Germany. Annual festivals celebrate his fifteen books about Winnetou and Old Shatterhand. Germans dress up as Apaches, build tepees, and re-enact his stories. Charles and Wesley's school is modeled on Dulwich College, a London boys' academy that remained open during the war, its teachers and students braving the Blitz with incredible pluck. The Union sharpshooter tragically killing his own son at the Battle of Malvern Hill is fact.

And if you hike in areas where there may be snakes, please carry a premade snakebite kit equipped with an extractor pump! Do NOT attempt the rescue Charles and Wesley did.

See www.lmelliott.com for more information.

Acknowledgments

Several librarians were a tremendous help to this novel's detail and authenticity. I am particularly indebted to Bill Barker, archivist of the Mariners' Museum in Newport News, who provided reams of documents about the Merchant Marine, Newport News docks, U-boats off our shores, and African Americans in wartime shipbuilding. Bill (and assistant archivist Bill Edwards-Bodmer) opened avenues to explore I hadn't even known existed. Thanks, too, to McLean High School's Joan McCarthy; St. Catherine School's Laura McCutcheon, and Tyler Paul; Mike Litterst of the National Park Service; Macs Smith for his research and German translations; and Captain Mike of www.discovertheJames.com, who introduced me to the James River's eagles and sturgeons, and to the place where Charles almost drowns.

Many friends helped: Dr. Howard Weeks edited scenes regarding hunting, quail, and general Southernisms. Illustrator/

author Henry Cole corroborated my memories of Virginia wildlife. Rowland Wilkinson kept my Briticisms "spot-on."

Editor Lisa Yoskowitz gently guided me in reining in tantalizing tangents that could have led Charles and Wesley's story astray, and in more clearly defining their personalities and demons. This novel is better given her deft touch.

My husband, John, a teacher who keeps the love of literature alive in teenagers, and Dr. Denise Ousley-Exum, who grooms fledging educators for that all-important job, reminded me of what captures the adolescent heart.

A real pleasure of this novel was reconnecting with my cousins Martha and Sarah, who enriched my painting of Tidewater Virginia. We spent a delightful afternoon along the James, laughing over stories about my grandparents and father, who inspired the characters of *Under a War-Torn Sky*, the first story in this World War II trilogy, and its sequel, *A Troubled Peace.*

Most important, as always, my children, Megan and Peter—who have grown up to be eloquent and insightful creative artists themselves—inspired me and then honed this novel through their repeated readings of its various stages of manuscript. Their adroit suggestions and questions quickened the novel's pacing, fleshed out its characters, plus deepened and chiseled its themes. Their influence permeates every page.